THORNE IN THE ROSE CITY

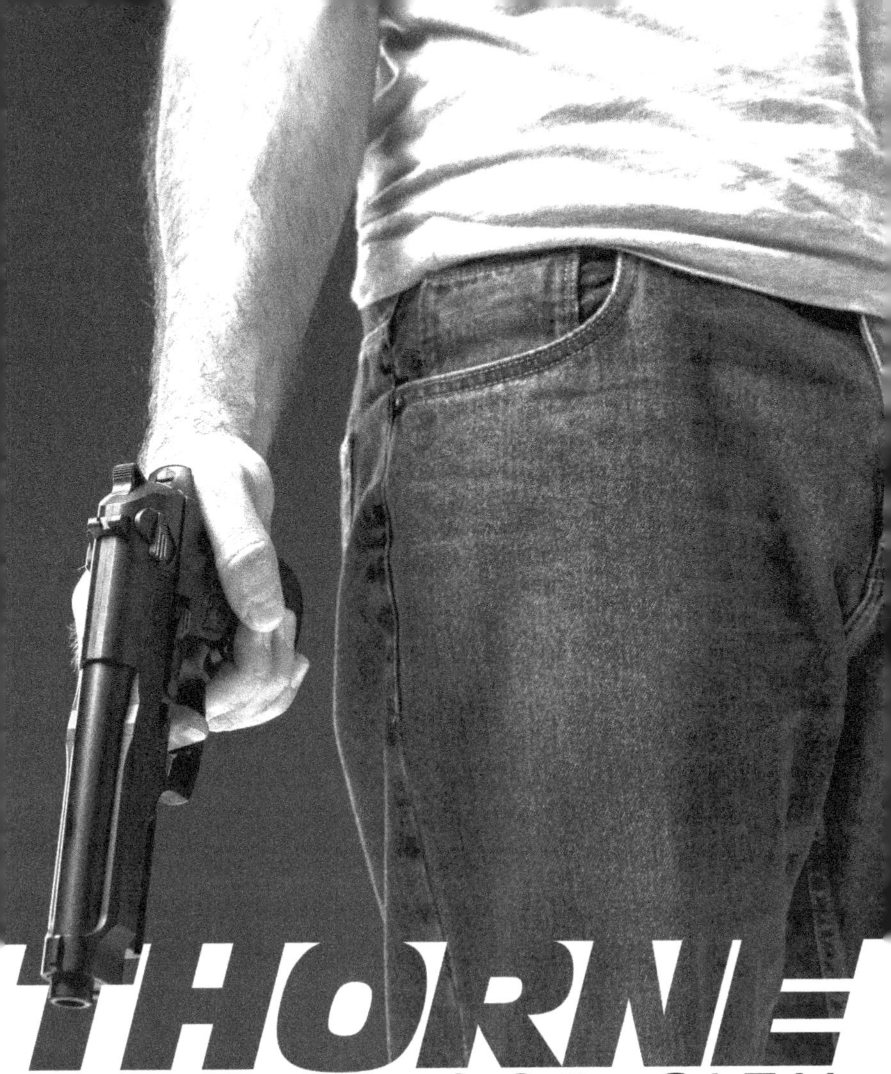

THORNE
IN THE ROSE CITY

BY
JUSTIN A. McWHIRTER

Copyright © 2019 by Justin A. McWhirter

Edited by Andrew Durkin
Cover and interior design by Masha Shubin
BigStockPhoto.com: Bandit © TomMisch; Portland © Yuri Konovalov; Bullet Holes © GoMixer.

This is a work of fiction. The events described here are imaginary. The settings and characters are fictitious or used in a fictitious manner and do not represent specific places or living or dead people. Any resemblance is entirely coincidental.

All rights reserved. No part of this book may be reproduced or transmitted in any form or by any means whatsoever, including photocopying, recording or by any information storage and retrieval system, without written permission from the publisher and/or author. The views and opinions expressed in this book are those of the author(s) and do not necessarily reflect those of the publisher, and the publisher hereby disclaims any responsibility for them. Neither is the publisher responsible for the content or accuracy of the information provided in this document. Contact Inkwater Press at inkwater.com. 503.968.6777

Publisher: Inkwater Press | www.inkwaterpress.com

Paperback ISBN-13 978-1-62901-633-7 | ISBN-10 1-62901-633-0
Kindle   ISBN-13 978-1-62901-634-4 | ISBN-10 1-62901-634-9

1 3 5 7 9 10 8 6 4 2

CHAPTER 1

IT'S REALLY EASY TO BE IN the city of Portland, Oregon and forget that the rest of the world exists. Aside from being the "hipster capital of the world" with its overt liberalism, the city is physically hemmed in by the massive western hills on one side of the river and another cluster of smaller buttes on the east; both are topped with tall fir trees to block the sight lines at the city limits. Once you're in the bowl of the Rose City, you can't see the reality outside. But like the waters of the Willamette River that slices through the town, the secrets Portland aims to keep to itself inside its bubble eventually squeeze out to the rest of the forgotten world. This is the lesson I was planning on teaching Pete Finn.

It had been five years since he took off with $40,000 from my employer in Hartford, Connecticut. He hadn't been heard from since.

Pete had been a good worker, running guns from Indiana to the Nutmeg State, where my employer was able to make a killing—to coin a phrase—by selling to the street gangs in Hartford's North End neighborhood. Despite being home to the Colt factory, Connecticut also has some of the strictest gun laws in the nation—but in a state like Indiana you can roll up to a gun show anywhere, drop a couple grand (spread out over a couple of vendors so you don't make a scene) and be back in New England twelve hours later. With the feds all keeping an eye on gun-smuggling runs from Georgia and Florida, the Indiana operations were bringing in plenty of green. So when Pete asked for forty grand to make another Hoosier run, the employer didn't think anything of it. Until Pete never came home, that is. That's when they got me on the case.

My name is Thorne, but don't bother looking for me in the yellow pages. Even if they had a listing for loan sharks I wouldn't register myself. I was born in New Haven, raised on the streets of Waterbury, and finally found my calling in the capitol city of Hartford. The only official documentation of me you'll find is a birth certificate and a newspaper clipping with the results of the 2008 New England Golden Gloves tournament. I reached the semifinals as a light heavyweight but never had the stuff to go pro. However, a life on the streets and a solid left hook made me a perfect candidate to track down those who still owed money to the employer and didn't want to be found.

So when I was tagged with finding Pete Finn,

it became infuriating that nothing ever turned up. I knew "Pete Finn" wasn't his real name. He used numerous aliases to keep himself under the radar of the ATF or any other federal group looking into him. I always figured he took the name from the gangster in Red Harvest but I never bothered to ask him. If the man used false names to hide himself he wouldn't tell you the truth about his real identity anyways. Still, for five years I plugged away at every alias of his I could think of, without any success.

People think tracking someone down is either low-tech legwork, like Sherlock Holmes—as if this was still Victorian times—or a quick hack job that they would see on CSI. The truth is much simpler and less sexy nowadays: Facebook, Instagram, and the old reliable: LexisNexis. People can't help but brag about how they exist in the world. You just have to know where to look.

Pete did a phenomenal job of hiding from me for five years, until he finally slipped up and his secret got out. Maybe he thought the employer in Hartford had forgotten about him. Maybe he had just spent too much time in Portland and succumbed to its ignorance that the rest of the world existed. Whatever it was, it didn't change the headline of the story in the Willamette Metro newspaper: "Portland Unity Coalition receives largest donation." The quick three-paragraph story—complete with a photo of the man who had run off with my employer's money—explained how Mr. Peter Finn had contributed $10,000 to the charity during their recent fundraising campaign, marking the biggest gift ever for the group.

LexisNexis was quick to find a Mr. Peter Finn listed at SE Seventy-Sixth Street in Portland, Oregon. No criminal record listed. No spouse or family living with him. Used an AT&T cellphone. The employer gave me strict instructions to catch the next flight to the West Coast and not come back until I had forty grand in hand.

That proved to be difficult, however—when I arrived at SE Seventy-Sixth Street, I found Pete sitting at his desk, with what looked like two .35 slugs in his chest. He'd been like that a few days already, judging by the dried blood on his shirt. Trying to get forty large from a dead man is much harder than getting it from a live one.

Pete's house was anything but noticeable. A forgettable little ranch painted a forgettable off-white, and wedged in a tight forgettable neighborhood. Inside the house, everything was organized in a middle-aged bachelor kind of way. It wasn't a total mess, but things seemed to be more organized by the way he would remember where they were than any traditional form. Books were on the shelves together by author, but the authors ran next to each other in no particular order. In the kitchen, beer glasses were next to big cooking pots, which were next to wine glasses. It was refreshing to see that five years and three thousand miles hadn't changed Pete at all.

It also gave me hope looking for Pete's notebooks. As a man who ran guns for a living, he never completely trusted computers. He'd watched too many episodes of Criminal Minds and figured the government could crack into his electronic files and spill the beans on his whole operation if they wanted to. He probably wasn't that far off. In any case, old school notebooks and pens were his world entirely.

A quick search didn't turn up anything, but I wasn't discouraged. It just meant that Pete was still as cautious as ever. He took pride in being a professional and wouldn't leave his ledgers lying around in the open. That's how Mandy Patinkin would have found them easy enough on the TV show. I started feeling around the desk that Pete was still sitting at, and found no locks on any of the drawers. The top one had nothing but pens, paper, and some loose staples. The bottom drawer was much deeper, and filled with worthless paperwork—rent on the house, electric bills. Boring.

It was when I cleaned out the papers that I hit pay dirt.

The drawer's wooden bottom had a similar wood-stained look as the rest of the desk, but was just off-color enough to be noticeable. I tried not touching Pete's body as I struggled to find a finger hold on the false bottom before finally giving it a few tugs. My reward was a beaten-up black-and-white composition notebook that seemed more appropriate for a doctoral candidate, rather than a gunrunner.

I gave it a quick look through, seeing lots of names and numbers crossed out. I decided it best to shorten my time in a house that was still being shared with an unreported corpse. I caught a nearby bus and found a dingy motel off Eighty-Second

Street—the kind of motel where you pay in cash and no one asks any questions. The manager already knew I was there to cheat on my wife so there was no reason to correct him.

Once in my room I poured myself a glass of White Label and dove into the business world of the infamous Pete Finn. Names and addresses were matched up, along with what was owed in both cash and product. What confused me were the amounts. Orders for five and six products I could figure, but the deals for twenty to forty—and even one for eighty—made me think either Portland had become the world's biggest hub for firearms or I was missing something. Although, figuring Pete had been here for five years, it wouldn't have surprised me if he had sold steel to everyone and their grandmother twice over in that time.

Through it all there was one name that kept popping up more than any other: "Scrubby Jim." No address, no phone number—just Scrubby Jim, over and over. I flipped open my laptop and a quick Google search came up with too many insignificant results to waste my time considering them just yet. Facebook turned up nothing either—but Instagram came through with flying colors: PDXScrubbyMan85. I don't know why he felt the need to add the "85," as I doubt there were eighty-four others lining up to be a "PDXScrubbyMan," but it did list underneath the screen name an account name as Jim Nichols. Now we were getting somewhere.

Back to Facebook. There were thirteen different accounts for Jim (or Jimmy) Nichols, but only one bragging that he was from the Rose City. The profile picture was of himself in midair, trying to pull an ollie on a skateboard. No clue if he landed it or not. He was wearing what looked like a leopard-print bathrobe—his dreadlocks held together by a bandanna wrapped around his forehead. He looked like Gary Oldman's character from True Romance. His photos on Instagram confirmed that I was looking at the right ScrubbyMan85. The guy was in deep in the notebooks of a gunrunner and was plastering himself all over social media, making him easy to find. Clearly not a professional. He might be itchy on the trigger if he'd been collecting guns from Finn. If I could keep him from shooting first, it would be easy to get answers out of him later.

LexisNexis put his last known address in the north quadrant of the city. Portland boasts of having five "quadrants"—not allowing math to affect how they name parts of the city. Just before midnight I rolled up to the small house wedged into another forgettable neighborhood and was greeted by a single light with a flashing television on in the front room. As I approached the door I could smell the strong stench of pot. I didn't even bother to check if the door was locked, and instead kicked it in with one strong effort.

"Holy shit! What the fuck man? What the fuck!"

No gunshots. I guess he was a "questions first" kind of guy. I walked in slowly. In my career hunting down those who owed money to the employer, I find that the only knowledge they have of people like me comes from the movies. And in the movies, it's always a hardcore badass who busts through the door and then starts breaking everything like a bat out of hell. Jet Li, Vin Diesel—it doesn't matter. Let the target think the worst and they'll do most of the work for you. ScrubbyMan85 proved to be no different.

Plus, he was stoned out of his mind.

"Jim Nichols," I said, as stoic as possible. I always liked to imagine myself as one of the ghosts haunting Ebenezer Scrooge. Not the little kid, but the one that looked like death, only if he could talk.

"What the fuck, man? You busted down my door, man. I just got that thing fixed."

"Fuck your door. You owe Pete Finn $800." It was an amount I remember seeing in the notebook next to the ScrubbyMan name.

"Pete Finn? Who the fuck is Pete Finn, man?"

"You owe someone $800 for guns and you don't even know who he is?"

"Guns? What are you talking about, man? I ain't got no guns. Why would I ever use a gun?"

"Don't fuck with me. You're stoned out of your mind but you can't weasel your way out of this."

"Look, man—I ain't got no guns. You can look around if you want. Shit, if I ever needed one, it was when that big-ass black man busted in here yesterday and tried to beat the shit out of me."

"What big-ass black man?"

"I told you, man—you busted my door I just got fixed. But he was only looking for $300 out of me. I didn't have it. Where are you getting $800 from, man?"

"He was looking for Pete's money?"

"Are you high, man? I told you, I don't know who Pete is. Are you sure you're in the right house?"

"I've seen True Romance—so yeah, I'm sure I'm in the right house."

"True Romance? Wait ... is that the chick flick with Cusack and that British girl?"

I finally couldn't hold my badass-ness in and gave a sigh of frustration. The only thing worse than a stoner was a stoner who was stupid even when sober. PDXScrubbyMan85 seemed to fit both of those categories. "If you aren't packing then why do you owe Pete the money?"

"I told you, man, I don't know anyone named Pete."

Finn had probably been using a different alias with Nichols.

He reached over to the coffee table and grabbed his bong, stuffing another pinch of weed in before taking a long drag that had the water bubbling almost to the point of no return. He looked up, holding the smoke in before finally letting out a long, satisfying exhale. I stood corrected. Jim was a professional—just not in anything criminal, since weed was now legal in Oregon. "Look, man. Here— just take a hit of this and everything will get better."

"Fuck that," I answered, and turned to storm out. "You'd better have the money within forty-eight hours," I demanded, knowing that it was an empty threat.

I slammed the door behind me on the way out, only to see someone waiting for me under the streetlight. It was a big-ass black man. Six foot and chiseled, with not a single muscle going to waste. He was rocking slightly baggy jeans with a plain white T-shirt that was tight enough to show off the work he had put in at the gym. I already knew he also had a killer jab-hook combination.

"Dynamite Anderson," I said. "What the hell are you doing here?"

"Thorne—you miserable son of a bitch. I could be asking you the same thing."

"You still drinking cheap bourbon? Or are you up for anything at this hour?"

"Beers are on you."

CHAPTER 2

I HAD FIRST MET DWAYNE "Dynamite" Anderson in the semifinals of the New England Golden Gloves. To be more specific, I met his right hook numerous times in the ring before I actually met the rest of him. But I could always take a good beating without going down, and I was the only fighter to take him to the judges on his way to winning the tournament.

Years later, I ran into him again in Hartford when he was helping out some mafia boys from Providence—they were trying to find a dealer peddling a batch of tainted heroin that had killed the big man's son. I was looking for the dealer too, for having skipped out on paying me twenty-five grand for some bodyguard work the previous year. Hartford's an open city, so even with an employer I didn't have any Mafiosos backing me, like Providence had provided Anderson. In the end, I found the dealer first—but the Providence boys conveniently misplaced his brains from the rest of his skull before I could get my money out of the guy. Providence paid me ten grand as a finder's fee and told me to keep my mouth shut. I guess you could call that a compromise.

"You're a long way from Connecticut," Anderson said, downing a PBR as we sat at a booth—the only patrons in a dimly lit bar that looked like it hadn't seen sunshine since the Bush administration. (Which Bush was open for debate.)

"And you're an even longer way from Little Rhody."

"First thing's last then. Why are you following me?"

"Following you? I figured you would probably be eating pasta somewhere after chasing down a Moses Brown kid right now, if I wasn't sitting here drinking with you."

That got a chuckle out of him. "Then what are you doing at that pothead's place?"

"You got to him first—why don't you tell me what you were doing there?"

Anderson thought about it for a moment but then cracked a smile. He was getting amusement out of winning our race to Nichols's house, even if neither of us knew that the competition was on. "I'm out here on a job from the big man in Providence. Some drug dealer back east skipped out on him with sixty grand, and then disappeared about five years ago. Only just recently his name pops up in some newspaper article and I get sent out here to find his ass."

"So you killed him?"

Anderson seemed startled. "What the hell are you talking about? You know me—I ain't in the killing business. There's plenty of the Providence boys who would love to get their start into that. I'm just the muscle but I don't do any of the killing."

"So you didn't kill Pete Finn?"

"By the time I got out here and found the house, Pete had taken two bullets to the chest. Wait ... how'd you know Pete was dead?"

"He skipped out on forty grand from my employer and disappeared for a couple of years. Then his name shows up in a newspaper article and, well, I think you can put the rest together from there."

"So Pete ripped off both Hartford and Providence in one swoop? Damn! The balls on that guy."

"Doesn't do him any good now. I'm supposed to bring back the money but unfortunately dead men have a hard time opening their wallets."

"Providence wanted him alive so they could give out their own brand of punishment. I told them they were out of luck and then got told to find his associates and make them the substitutes."

Some of the pieces were starting to come together. I always wondered why Pete would have skipped out of Hartford for only $40,000, but if he had another $60,000 involved that might make a man have big enough delusions of grandeur to escape to the West Coast. Still—that one answer didn't make up for the five more questions that followed.

"What made you think Nichols was one of his associates?" I asked. "Pete was always a smart guy.

I don't think he would have chosen to work with a worthless stoner like that."

"Found his name in a notebook. Paid him a visit, and when I didn't get the answers I wanted I decided to stake the place out to see who would show up. Turns out the next person was you."

"What notebook?"

"Pete's notebook." Anderson reached into a bag and pulled out a blue and black composition notepad, throwing it on the table. It was an exact twin of the notebook I had in my possession except for the cover being a different color. "That asshole Nichols—or should I say 'Scrubby Jim'—kept popping up. Some moniker Nichols goes by. I found his real name and address and then decided to bust down the door. You didn't think you could break through that all by yourself did you? You know how to take a punch, but you weren't the best at dealing out the punishment compared to the rest of us in the division."

"I made the semifinals. That means something."

"Yeah, it means that no one likes a fucking southpaw. You guys are the worst."

I couldn't help but crack a smile. "What else did you find in this notebook?"

"I haven't been able to decipher it all yet, but there's something weird with it. The sales don't match up. It's all incredibly low numbers. Two or three units of whatever at a time. The Pete I knew would have been selling in higher numbers for a heroin dealer."

"That's the second time you've called him a drug dealer."

"Yeah—so?"

"He wasn't a drug dealer."

"Pete Finn? Hell yeah he was. Or at least a drug runner. He dealt in big shipments. Had some connections with a Mexican cartel in Michigan. Guy would drive up there himself and come back with kilos all nicely packed. Providence and the cartel didn't completely trust each other so Pete was the perfect go between."

"That motherfucker!" I let out.

"What?"

"Finn was the gunrunner for Hartford—and he was good at it, too. He would drive out to Indiana and pick up full shipments at all those right-wing nut-job gun shows, run by those Second-Amendment-loving country hicks who don't ask questions just in case big bad Obama was listening."

"So he'd drive to Indiana for the guns ..."

"And then stop in Michigan to meet the Mexicans. He probably had a trunk full of guns when he did it."

"Nothing wrong with a little insurance in the trunk just in case the cartel changed their minds."

"Not with guns he bought with the employer's money. Fuck. If he weren't already dead I'd give serious thought to beating him to death myself ... wait. You said you didn't kill him either, right?"

"He was dead when I broke into the house," Anderson said. "I looked around and found the notebook on the desk. I took it and decided to go through it somewhere else."

"And that's where you came across Nichols's name?"

"Yeah, I told you that. How'd you get to Nichols?"

"Fucking Pete. He was dealing in heroin and guns separately. You took the blue notebook and left. You didn't look at the false bottom of the desk drawer. That's the notebook you were looking for."

"How can you tell?"

"Because it made no sense to me that he was selling in such large numbers. You got his guns book. I got his heroin book."

"And Nichols was in both of them?"

"What's a professional pothead like him doing with heroin and guns?" I asked.

"Maybe we should go ask him."

"Is this a partnership you're suggesting?"

"I just need a live body to bring back to Providence."

"As long as I can get forty grand out of it you can have your body and make everyone happy."

"What makes you think you can still get the money from a dead man?"

"Just look at the numbers. Between the guns and the heroin, Pete was pulling in a pretty good take—but you saw his house. Small yet just slightly comfortable, filled with only the things he really needs to live. No Ferrari, no party yacht. Pete liked to stay under the radar, even if he was bringing in a lot of cash. The only thing we know he spent was ten grand to that Unity Group of Portland—"

"Portland Unity Coalition."

"Whatever. We've got two books that say he made plenty more than just five figures. The question is—where did it go?"

"Maybe he was a Good Samaritan and decided to spread out his wealth." Anderson took another drink. "You know—ten grand to the Unity Coalition, fifteen to the Cub Scouts. Maybe twenty-five to the ASPCA. Who can say no to Sarah McLachlan?"

"The man sold guns and drugs while dealing with Providence mobsters and Mexican cartels. Something tells me he isn't one to dedicate his life to saving puppies."

"All right, then where's the cash? You want me to go get a shovel and start digging up his backyard? It might bring some unwanted attention. An unknown brother digging up the backyard of a man still lying dead inside. Hell, just being dark skinned will draw attention to me. I haven't seen a city this pale in my life."

"And you're from Rhode Island," I couldn't help but point out.

"Damn straight. So what's the plan then?"

"Well we've only got two leads at the moment, and since you've already proven to be quite adept at keeping an eye on our dear Mr. ScrubbyMan, why don't you keep watch to see who else might be kicking down his door?"

"And what will you be doing while I'm taking care of that exciting job?"

"I'm going to set up a meeting with the Unity Coalition and find out why Pete was dropping so much dough with them."

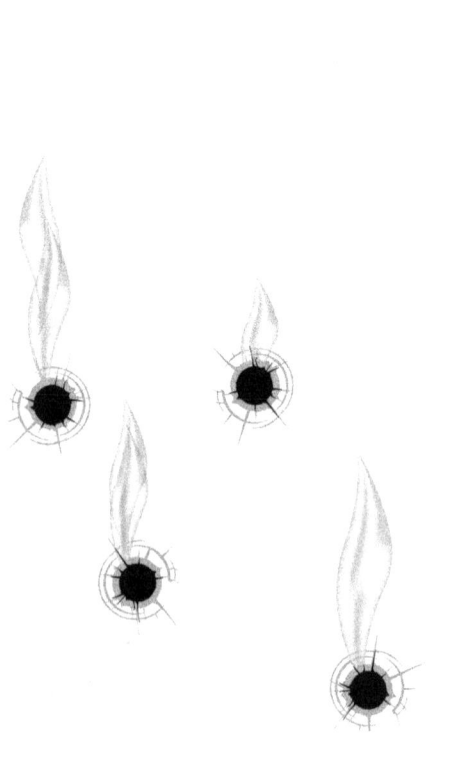

CHAPTER 3

THAT MORNING I GOT myself an afternoon appointment with Ms. Nancy Burkhart, the head of the Portland Unity Coalition. I claimed to be a freelance journalist working on a story about money-laundering schemes involving innocent charities like hers. She seemed hesitant, so I gave my name as Carter Williams and gave her a moment to look me up. Williams had published a few freelance stories in smaller papers from New Haven to Baltimore, so when she looked up the name, and it appeared to prove what I was telling her, it would calm some fears. This wasn't my first rodeo. A real reporter once told me the trick to getting a story is to get the target to believe in you enough that they start telling the real story whether they mean to or not. That and a shitload of LexisNexis research. Turns out I probably could have made a great reporter except for the whole writing thing. The play has worked before where I have claimed to be a small-time freelance writer as an alibi, and this time it got Mr. Carter Williams an appointment with the head of the Portland Unity Coalition.

The place was a tiny storefront wedged on Cesar Chavez Boulevard just off Hawthorne. Close enough to the heart of the city to pretend that they are making a difference with the hipster one-love culture center of Portland while still far enough away to be able to pay the rent. The staffing looked to match that frugal concept as Ms. Burkhart was the only one in the office when I arrived.

"Mr. Williams, I presume?" she asked, with an air of arrogance fueled by pure unfiltered contempt for my inconveniencing her day. She rocked a perfume that punched you in the face—while you were gasping for breath, she was in control of the situation and not taking shit from anybody. She sat behind a small, cheap metal desk that seemed to be an extension of her. On the wall behind her were a few certificates of appreciation for the work of the coalition. One small framed photograph looked like it had been taken nearly twenty years ago, and showed a white man and a black man posing like best buds, smiling with their arms around each other. It was like one big happy family—evidence of why the icy cold woman in front of me got all those certificates.

"Ms. Burkhart," I said, trying my best charming smile. It sucked. She offered me a seat across from her desk. I gladly took it and finished off my image by taking out a notepad and a small tape recorder I had bought from a retro electronics shop down the street.

"You know phones today all come with audio recording apps," she sneered from behind the metal desk.

"I can never completely trust those things. The memory could fill up, or a file get corrupted. I'm old school and like my tapes." I wanted to applaud myself for how good I was at the reporter act. "Just for clarity's sake, what is the mission of the Portland Unity Coalition?"

"We work with other groups within the greater Portland area to create opportunities that bring harmony and togetherness for all people in our fine city." She sounded like she was reading it right off a brochure.

"And by harmony and togetherness you mean anyone from Portland?"

"Yes, we are open to all people, no matter their race or creed or origin."

"And this is to achieve that goal of making everyone equal in the most positive of ways, for your most progressive of future ideals?"

"Let's cut right through the shit, Mr. Williams. I find it incredibly insulting that you would fly all the way across the country just to sit down with me and tell me to my face that you think there is something fishy going on with my organization. This is my life's work, Mr. Williams. I've given everything to the coalition—so insulting it is insulting me personally."

"It is not so much yourself I am looking into, Ms. Burkhart, but a donor of yours. Do you know a man named Pete Finn?"

She hesitated for a moment—that told me more

than if she had actually said anything. "Who are you, really, Mr. Williams?"

"I told you, I am a freelance journalist—"

"Cut the bullshit. I tried doing some research on you this morning and came up with very little. Oh, sure—I found a fluff piece on the Yale graduation from a few years ago, but nothing that actually identifies you. No Facebook, no LinkedIn profile, no Twitter handle. What kind of a journalist doesn't have one of those?"

"Have you seen the kind of comments that reporters and journalists are getting in Trump's America? When you put your name on news nowadays it just invites the crazies and the racists to threaten your family on every kind of digital platform. It doesn't even matter that I'm not married and don't have kids—the crazies still claim to be coming for them. No, thank you. I'll keep my name in the byline, and that's it."

Boom. This cowboy could go eight seconds on any ride she brought out.

"And I'm supposed to believe you flew out here—today, of all days?"

"What's so special about today?"

"If you're a reporter who just flew in from the East Coast, then what's the color of the carpet at PDX?"

"Blue." I could tell she was trying to call out my bluff so I had no problem making it seem like I was holding all the cards.

She took a moment to try and compose herself, taking a deep breath. Some humanity began to come through in her voice. "You see Mr. Williams,

I got a phone call at seven this morning, alerting me that Pete Finn was found dead in his house. Shot and killed probably a few days ago, though no one found him until this morning. Three hours later I get a call from a snooping journalist looking for information on a donation Mr. Finn gave to the coalition a few weeks ago."

"You said he's dead?" I tried to play innocent.

"That's all the police told me when they called up asking questions. Turns out Mr. Finn doesn't have any immediately known next of kin, and my name came up due to the donation, so they asked if I had any information."

"And?"

"And it's a conversation I had with the police, not with a questionable journalist. A good man was just murdered. Can't you allow him a few moments of respect before you start trying to make a bigger name for yourself with a character assassination piece—since you're snooping around asking about money-laundering cases in organizations like my own?"

"Do you know what kind of person Pete Finn really was?" I leaned back in my chair and asked sternly.

"What is that supposed to imply?"

"It's supposed to imply that while tracking him, I've come across evidence that he dropped donations using numerous aliases and fake accounts."

"What evidence?"

"I can tell you that Mr. Finn moved to the greater Portland area within the last five years. At least, that's if he's been using the name Pete Finn that whole time. I've also tracked him to accounts in the names of Donald Willsson, Max Thaler, and Reno Starkey. So how did he donate to you?"

The anger in her sparked back to life. "He donated to the coalition as Mr. Peter Finn. He provided a driver's license, bank routing number—hell, even a passport—and suggested we do another fundraiser in British Columbia. If that's not good enough for you, then I think you'd best get to DC and have a word with the government about the shitty job they're doing in cracking down on identity fraud."

"How many times did Mr. Finn donate to the coalition then?"

"I'm not sure I like the line of this questioning. Do you have a warrant to go diving into my books?" She kept herself stoic behind her metal desk as if she were guarding the castle from an invader.

"No ma'am, I'm just a simple reporter looking—"

"Looking to ruin a man's name hours after he turns up dead, and ruining my life's work for being associated with someone you claim is a fraud and a crook with no evidence to show for it. I will not have any of it. Our time here is done."

"I am just trying to get answers for a story. You can't stop the power of the press. If not me, it'll be someone else."

"I'm not worried about the power of the press coming from you. The carpet at PDX is famous for being green. So next time you show up here pretending to be a reporter know that I'm calling the police to take you away, and I won't have any guilty conscience about denying your First Amendment rights, Mr. ... not Williams. Now get the fuck out of my office."

I grabbed the tape recorder and shut it off, putting it away in my pocket. "Pete took two slugs to the chest. He owed a lot of people a lot of money. It wasn't me that killed him, but it might have been the next person who shows up at your office. After all, he's on record for making a donation your way without any next of kin to speak of. Food for thought. Thank you for your time, Ms. Burkhart."

I smiled again and walked out.

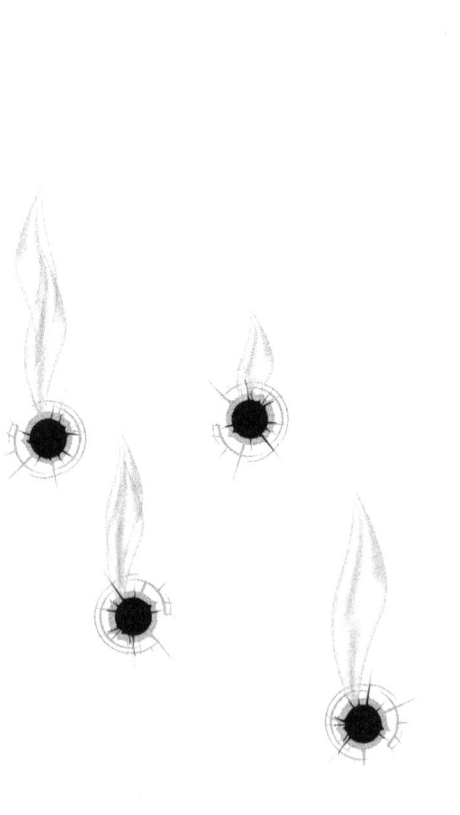

CHAPTER 4

"SHE SAW RIGHT THROUGH you."

Anderson was laughing as he cracked open another PBR. Right after leaving my afternoon meeting with Ms. Burkhart, I had bought a six-pack as a peace offering, and took it to the north quadrant, where Dynamite was now sitting in a car across the street from the Nichols house to keep watch on the place. I had joined him in the car, sliding into the passenger seat and grabbing a beer for myself.

"Yeah, but there's something up with her."

"You mean besides being a bitch?" Dynamite asked.

"Well, that doesn't help. She's running a small-time public benefit charity that clearly needs all the money it can get, and yet she's a stone-cold bitch. That's not exactly the warm and fuzzy type that people want to open their checkbooks to."

"Pete did."

"Yeah—and for a lot. I mean, that check alone probably kept the office open for most of the year."

"And what does this group do again?"

"Creates opportunities for harmony and togetherness for something that helps a thing or whatnot."

"Sounds rather vague."

"Intentionally vague."

"Maybe she figured a real reporter like you would have done your research and already known what the group does," Anderson chuckled.

"I guess I deserve that."

"I especially like the part on the tape where you reeled off his other aliases. Max Thaler? Donald Willsson? I've never heard Pete use those names."

"I know, but I just got in the moment. I haven't had a chance to check her story that she's only known Pete as Pete Finn, but I think she might have been telling the truth. Think about it—we always knew Pete used so many fake names in his dealings that we never gave any thought to if he was ever using a real name. What if his name was actually Pete Finn, and we just didn't care?"

"The more identities a man has, the more they express the person they conceal."

"What the hell is that?"

Anderson shrugged. "Read it in a book once. One of those quotes I've always kept to memory just for the moment I could use it to make myself sound smart." He took another long sip of his beer without taking his eyes off the front door of the house. "So do you think there's a connection between Burkhart and Pete?"

"Well, there's something. You don't just drop ten grand to a stranger, with a vague purpose."

"You do if you're trying to run a money-laundering operation."

"Yeah, that crossed my mind too. You don't get too many bank accounts or credit card orders for guns and drugs. That would be a lot of cash Pete was working with. A vague charity that's small enough to escape the attention of the IRS would be a damn good scheme. Kind of upset the employer didn't think of that back east."

"What proof do you have that's the game?"

"Jack squat outside of the fact that she seemed a little jumpy when I mentioned money-laundering as my made-up excuse for setting up a meeting with her. But she could be jumpy for other reasons." I killed off my beer and reached for another. "I'll have to think of something."

"What, like prove it's a laundering scheme and then blackmail her for forty grand so you don't expose her? If Pete was bringing in even more money than that, and with him not having any next of kin to pass the inheritance on to, she might still come up ahead and play ball with you."

"Something like that. I'll have to polish the idea a little more first."

"You'll have to polish it real nice and shiny. I checked in with the big man in Providence and told him the situation when you were in your meeting. He said if I can't bring him a body, then the sixty grand would do instead."

"So now I have to try and blackmail a stone-cold

bitch out of six figures and hope that it still leaves enough for her to go along with it?"

"Like I said, you'd best get polishing."

I gave a frustrated sigh and tried to change the subject. "What's our boy been up to today? I'll put the over/under at four bowls smoked."

"No clue," Anderson said. "I doubt he's even in there. I haven't seen him all day."

"Then what the hell have you been doing?"

"Keeping an eye on the place from here in the car. I haven't seen anything stir the whole time. Pothead or not, if you've had two big-ass Golden Glovers kick through your door on back-to-back nights, you'd hightail it the fuck out of there. He probably bolted last night after you left."

"Have you gone up to the house to check?"

"Not while it's still daylight. If he is in there, he's probably eyeing every window of the house and now has himself armed with something from Pete. Nope, I ain't going up there until nightfall—but like I said, I doubt he's in there."

"Then why are we staying here?"

"Where else do you want me to go?" Anderson asked. "The only lead we've got is Nichols, and the only place we know where he's been is right here. It's pointless to try and track him in a city I don't know to a place I have no clue he could be at. Nah, we'll stay here and see what pops up. Maybe he comes back. Maybe someone else comes for him."

"You mean like if Pete could rip off Hartford and Providence he might have made a play with the Winter Hill gang too?"

"If he had been in bed with those Southies at the same time as working for Providence, the big man would long ago have sliced him to bits and fed him to his crew, saying it was chowder."

"We didn't know he was working for both of us."

"That's different. Providence is a set crew. Hartford is just your employer and he's not really a crime boss. More like a crime landlord, if you know what I mean."

"Yeah, I get you. He's got just me and Providence has ... well, there were four guys with you last time I think."

"And don't let their size fool you. I'm easily the biggest of them, but my job was always just to look the scariest. Those little Italian guys who seem innocent enough like to take pleasure in killing sometimes."

I took another drink and looked around the neighborhood. "So if not Boston, who else will be coming for Nichols?"

"That's what we've got to find out. Patience, man. Well, that and another six-pack. You keep an eye on the place—I need to go stretch my legs with a beer run." He slapped me on the shoulder before laughing again. "Ha ha ... the carpet is green. Man, she owned you!"

"Just get something besides PBR."

It was the only thing I could think to yell out. He was right—I had gotten totally owned.

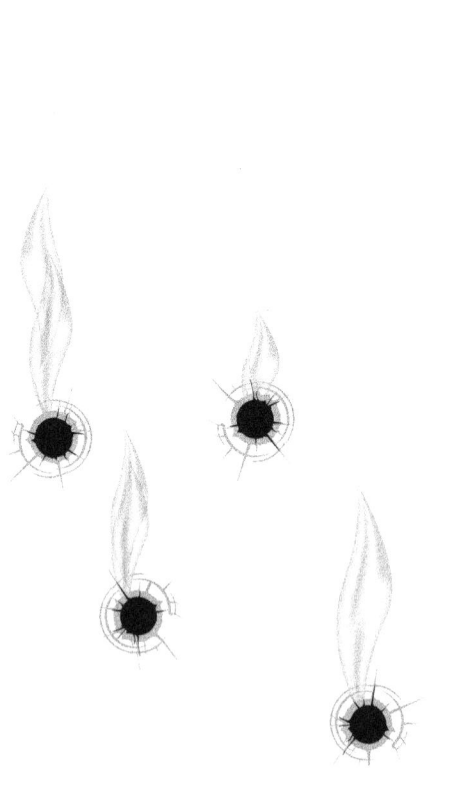

CHAPTER 5

IT TURNS OUT WE DIDN'T need to have patience for very long. Once the sun finally set and it was dark enough, I kept watch while Anderson crept up to the house to have a look around. Just as he thought, the place was empty. Nichols had hightailed it out of there before a third person came busting through his door. He remembered to take his bong but very little else.

So it was back to the waiting game and to see if by chance any other party decided to pay a visit to the pothead. Anderson and I decided to split into shifts. He lost the coin toss, and I let him take the kickoff and went back to my dingy motel from some sleep. Just as I had finally gotten into a dream about myself playing for the Whalers, my burner phone went off, dragging me back to the land of the living. The alarm clock on the nightstand shone

1:08 a.m. in harsh red digits. Still in a daze, I asked, "Anderson, what's up?"

"You've got to get your ass back here."

"Why? Something happen?"

"Yeah, something happened."

"You on the run?"

"Nah, I don't think anyone saw me outside of the guy that was trying to break into the place."

"Where's he now?"

"Gone, like the wind. I took his gun though."

"He came at you with a gun?"

"It wasn't for me but I still took it off of him. There's more to it, though."

"Like what?"

"Like the gun's a .35."

"A .35? Shit. Are you suggesting that you're holding the gun that likely killed Pete?"

Anderson sighed. "My guess is that I am. We're cool for now but get down here and help me clean this mess up."

I threw on the same clothes I had been wearing before and hopped a Lyft ride back to the house. Anderson was waiting for me in his car a few blocks down the road, just in case anyone had heard the scuffle at Nichols's place and decided to call the cops. He was still a little hopped up from the action and had a pair of battle scars. One was a slight slash on the side of his head that was still leaking a little, and the other was a small cut on the knuckle that showed the kind of battle scars the owner of the .35 was sure to be sporting.

"Start from the beginning," I told Anderson as I sat in the car and closed the door.

"It must have been around eleven or so. I was sitting in the car in the same spot, keeping an eye on the place like before, when I heard a noise rattling from behind the house. The neighborhood is pretty quiet at night so the noise was a little startling—I'm surprised no one else went to check it out."

"A rattling noise isn't important enough of a reason to get out of bed and I don't think this is a big call-the-cops kind of neighborhood."

"Fair enough—but it still was enough for me to check out. I crept around back and found this guy trying to pick the lock on a window—but the way he was making a mess of it he was more likely to just break through the whole glass before beating the lock."

"What did he look like?"

"Scrawny white guy. Maybe five foot five. I couldn't guess a weight in the dark but couldn't have been anything over a middleweight."

"And he gave you that present on the side of your head?"

"Let me get to that part. So I let the guy work a little longer before finally confronting him in case someone finally decided to call the cops. 'Nichols ain't home,' I told him. Well, that spooked the shit out of him. He turned and instantly threw a punch without even looking, and missed wildly. This guy was clearly out of his league so I decided to play it cool.

"'Who the fuck are you?' he asked.

"'Nichols' guardian angel. Who the fuck are you?'

"Well he didn't seem to like that answer at all and decided to make a run for it back around the house. I took off after him but when I came around the corner he pulled the gun and had it pointing right at me—only the guy was pure amateur. His hand was shaking from nerves and he probably wouldn't have hit me even if he had emptied the clip. I made my move and gave him a solid combo. One to the face, two quick to the body, and then finish with a left hook."

I rubbed my face, thinking of long-healed bruises of my own. "I remember that combination well."

"I missed the finisher though because he was falling toward me, trying to grapple me to the ground. We wrestled for a moment when he brought down the gun on the side of my head. I was stunned for a moment but was still able to grab the barrel and make sure it was pointed away from me—just in case. In that moment he let go of the gun and took off. For being a terrible burglar, the guy had speed. I chased him through a couple of backyards when I saw him diving into an old P.O.S. Oldsmobile."

"I didn't know they even still had those on the road."

"Neither did I. By the time I got to the car he had turned the engine and was about to take off. Still I gave a solid stomp kick to the back bumper to try and scare him—but in pure P.O.S. style the whole bumper fell from the rest of the car. He took off with the busted-up Olds and disappeared. That's when I called you and now you're up to date."

"Wait—you chased him to the car and all you did was kick the bumper off?"

"Yeah."

"What the hell does that do? Now all we've got is a broken bumper of some guy—who, like Nichols, certainly ain't coming back here. We're back to square one. Hell, we're even farther away, since all of our leads have come and gone."

"Not necessarily."

"Not necessarily? Did you forget to mention that you traded business cards? Are you now following each other on Twitter?"

"We've got the bumper."

"Is his name on the thing?"

"No, but I had an idea. I pulled this trick on a target back in New Bedford once and it worked beautifully. He never saw it coming."

"And what trick is that?"

Anderson pulled out his phone and started typing a website into it quickly. "What do you know about cars?"

"Four wheels, an engine, and Italian ones go real fast."

"They stopped making Oldsmobiles back in the mid-2000s. My older brother was a shop mechanic and used to work on them all the time. All those old New England grandparents used to drive the things until they were too blind to get behind the wheel, and then would pass them on to their grandkids to mess up. He used to get a ton of them into the shop and would let me help work on them. To my eye that P.O.S. our mystery guest had was either a '96 or '97

Cutlass Supreme. And to be honest, with how easily that bumper came off I'm surprised the rest of the car would still be running in such a bad condition."

"What does this have to do with anything?"

"2004 was the last year they made the Cutlass Supreme, which also means it was the last year they made parts for it. Our friend tonight might have been a shitty burglar but he was still a burglar. The last thing he would want is for the police to pull him over for driving without a bumper and then find out he's on a warrant, or has crack in the car, or something like that. It means he'll need to find a bumper—and quick—if he still wants to get around."

"So where does he go to get a bumper? There must be dozens of shops around Portland."

"We don't have to go to any of them," he said, smiling gleefully as he pushed the last button on the phone and turned it to show me the screen. "I just posted an ad on Craigslist for cheap parts for a mid-90s Cutlass Supreme. I said the engine blew out and it's worthless to try and repair the whole thing so I might as well sell off all the pieces. All we have to do now is wait for him to come to us looking for a bumper."

I gave him a look of disbelief. "You can't be serious."

"I told you, it worked before in New Bedford."

"What makes you think it'll work again?"

"Craigslist is a wonder. It's the first place people go to look for junk they need. Besides, we don't have any other leads. Let's give this a few days to soak. In the meantime we'll keep an eye on Nichols's place just in case unless you've got any other great ideas."

He was right—we were grasping at straws at this point. Waiting for our friend to check in looking for a bumper was better than doing nothing.

"What makes you think he might be connected to Nichols?" I asked. "Maybe he's just a random burglar looking for a score. Nichols is a big-time pothead, and from Pete's book probably involved in some kind of heroin. A quick peek inside shows no one is in the house. Any burglar would find this a perfect time to hit the place of a guy who likely has money around."

"Not this guy. He was way out of his league. If this was a burglar looking to score he would have tried the first window, found it locked, and then moved on to the second window. Our friend tonight was something else. He was trying to get into the house with the gun, not to get out with cash or anything like that."

I took the gun from Anderson and looked it over. "No way to tell if this was the weapon that killed Pete, but it is a .35. It could just be a coincidence, but I never like coincidences. That's just lazy thinking."

"I never like them either," Anderson said. "But since my fingerprints are all over this thing now I'm going to get rid of it."

"Where are you going to do that?"

"This city has a ton of bridges. I think the river is deep enough to take care of the situation."

I opened the door and got out of the car. "You deal with that. I'll find a post here and keep an eye out just in case."

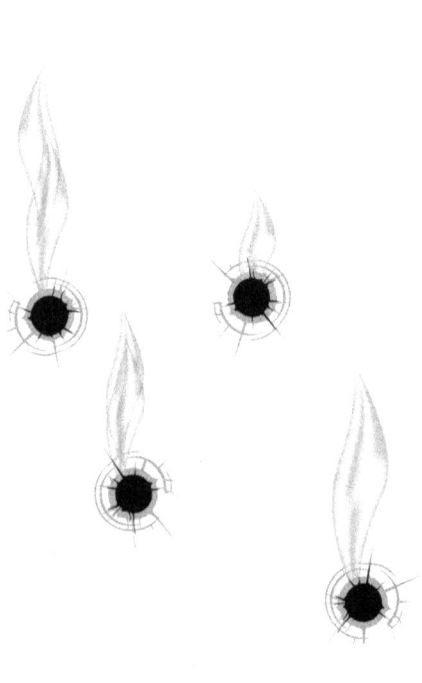

CHAPTER 6

IT TOOK ALL OF TWO DAYS before we finally got the email we were waiting for. We'd already gotten a couple of replies to the Craigslist ad, but we knew they weren't from our guy. Kevin from Beaverton was looking for the front panels and asked about the condition of the original color. Two requests came for the cloth seats—from folks who were trying to rebuild their old cars for their kids. I told them we'd already sold the seats.

Finally we got the email request for the back bumper. The writer asked if it was in good enough condition for him to drive around without being pulled over by the police. Sounded like our guy. The email even came in with an address that sounded generic, but was just specific enough to belong to a real person: NordicHammer95.

Back at my motel I popped open the computer. But Facebook and Twitter didn't come up with anything that matched the screen name at all, and without some kind of actual identification or address the magic of LexisNexis was useless. It was Instagram that came through again—but not in the way we were expecting.

The photo app didn't come up with a NordicHammer95 but did pull up the Knights of the Nordic Hammer. One click on the screen name brought up a whole host of group shots with ten to twenty white men in each, all with buzzed or extremely trimmed hair. Most of the photos had the members proudly holding up red flags with a white circle and a black Celtic cross in the middle. They were white-power skinheads.

In some photos, a few group members proudly displayed their new swastika tattoos, while others flexed in their white tank tops to show off the Nazi SS lightning symbols inked across their chests. There were only white men—none more than thirty-five years old. Almost all of them wore tank tops, black jeans, and boots that screamed how they were steel-toed and could mess someone up in a bar fight.

"Look at these shitheads," I said, passing the laptop over to Anderson. He scrolled through the images with his normal tough-guy face, not showing any emotion besides something between anger and disgust.

"Never would have guessed something like this would be in Portland. I thought this city was all about pride and love and yearning for Bernie Sanders."

"I guess there's a few bad apples everywhere."

"But I never would think Portland had white supremacists."

"A couple of years ago I had to go after this guy from Wallingford who didn't pay up his tab. You know Wallingford? It's this little perfect suburban town halfway between Hartford and New Haven. Boy Scouts, bake sales, everything you'd imagine. Only it turns out the guy was some kind of grand wizard for the town's Klan group. Yeah, they had the robes and everything. I don't know if they did any of the Jim Crow cross-burning stuff, but apparently they'd go to other local towns—places like Cheshire and Wolcott—and hold up their supremacist bullshit signs. It would be six of them in their robes with the hoods down thinking they were going to change the world because they were shouting things at passing motorists in front of the town hall. How do you deal with someone like that? They don't live on a logical plane like the rest of us, so you can't even talk to them. I asked where's the money he owes the employer and the guy goes on some rant about how the Jews are the ones to blame because they run the economy in order to get revenge on what he called real Americans."

"Did you get the money?"

"Eventually. Guys like this are almost all talk and no action. They know they don't have any backing so they scream their heads off thinking it makes them sound powerful enough where no one will call them out on it. But show up with a couple of left hooks and even six of them ain't worth a dime, robes or no robes."

"No one likes a southpaw."

"Ain't heard much from the Wallingford crew

after that though. Got my money and did a little civic duty in the process. I think that counts as good use of being a lefty."

"Yeah but those were Klansmen hiding under their robes because they saw Birth of a Nation once and listened to too much country music," Anderson said, still looking closely at the Instagram account. "These guys look different. No hoods. Hell, they're trying to show off how tough they are by taking turns posing with that one assault rifle. Look, it's the same weapon in every picture but with different people holding it like they're trying to make it seem as if they have a much larger gun collection. Still, I don't think they're the kind of all-talk bullshit you had in Wallingford. The Nordic Hammer here on the right practically says they're ready for a fight and they'll ..." He paused for a second before exclaiming, "That motherfucker!"

"What is it?"

"That scrawny little motherfucker," he said again, turning the laptop back to show me. He pointed at another picture of fifteen members of the group standing in two columns holding up another of the racist red flags with the black cross in the middle. "Top row, third from the left. That's him."

"That's who?"

"That's our burglar."

"The guy who hit you over the head with the gun?"

"The guy who's missing a bumper on a P.O.S. Cutlass."

"Are you sure? It was dark and he did scramble your vision with the hit to the head."

"Of course I'm sure. That's him. Nordic-Hammer95 has to be our guy." Anderson pushed his finger against the picture and up popped a number of different names listed as Instagram accounts that were tagged to each person. One click on the screen name to the third guy from the left took us to the account of Tyler Dixon. There he was in a number of more normal pictures: enjoying a beer at the bar, on a hunting trip in Idaho, and playing an electric guitar in front of a similar red flag—but with his mighty Gibson axe blocking the cross logo in the middle of the white circle.

"I'm going to reply to the Craigslist email and set up a meeting with him to give him a sequel of our previous encounter," Anderson said.

"Hold on—let's think about this first," I said. "What is an unabashed white supremacist doing trying to break into Nichols's house? I mean, Nichols is a white guy. Painfully white."

"Maybe he was in their group?"

"Unlikely. You met the guy—he was so stoned. He gave off that laziness vibe. You really have to be focused to hate people enough to join a supremacist group, and Nichols didn't seem like he had been focused on anything since 2005."

"Well, he was wrapped up in Finn's gun and heroin dealings. Maybe he was working with the Nordic Hammers."

"If he was working with them then why send one guy to break into the house?"

"So you're thinking he was a rival of some kind?"

"I don't know. If the whole group was after

Nichols, then why send only one guy—and Dixon in particular? I mean, look at the rest of the group—there's at least a dozen other guys who look more ripped than our man. Shit—he's even holding the rifle wrong in the picture. He probably thinks he's looking tough, but really he's just showing off that he don't know anything. You said yourself that he was a pure amateur holding the .35 the night he tried to break into the house. If they wanted to kill Nichols, why send this guy?"

Anderson took a minute to think it over before saying, "But Finn was probably done with the same gun, and that was a professional job. Two in the chest, no sign of a fight—he was probably taken by surprise. No way it was Dixon."

"So the group is taking turns doing its dirty business. Maybe the planned attack on Nichols was trying to blood in this guy to the group?"

"So it was Finn and Nichols against the Nordic Hammers?"

"But why? Neither of them was even close to being a minority."

"Finn only cared about money, never what racial group it came from. I told you he was dealing with the Mexicans when running heroin back to Providence."

"So maybe he was killed for working with Mexicans?"

"Nah. If I was a white supremacist I'd kill a Mexican for being a drug dealer, but skip out on a white guy dealer who happened to be working with the Mexicans as a sign to the cartels working the area.

Skip over the middle man with my hate. Maybe the Hammers were dealing heroin themselves and Finn and Nichols were cutting in on their profits."

"That's starting to make sense," I agreed. I was busy on my laptop going through Facebook first and looking for Tyler Dixons across America. A number of them popped up with a popular name like that, but none were in Portland, and none were with pictures of our guy. Twitter brought up nothing as well. It was up to LexisNexis, and that came through in fine fashion.

"Find anything on this guy yet?" Anderson asked as he paced around the motel room, anxious to make a move on his assailant.

"And then some. Mr. Tyler Dixon has a house in a place called Detroit, Oregon."

"Where the hell is that?"

"The map here puts it up in the mountains, maybe an hour or so away. Looks devoid of civilization."

"Sounds like the place a white supremacist group would like to call home."

"I doubt there's very many Oldsmobile Cutlasses up there. Seems more like pickup-truck territory."

"Forget setting up a time to meet with him—if we've got his address, let's drop by and finish what I started."

"Slow down there. We need to talk to the guy first and figure out how he's connected to Nichols to be connected to Finn. If Nichols has some kind of involvement in white supremacist groups, whether or not that's why these Nordic Hammers wanted to kill him, and we know we can connect Nichols to

Finn through the notebooks, that would work nicely in blackmail material for someone running a unity coalition like Ms. Burkhart. Once we figure that out and get the money for the bosses back east, you can finish things with our boy Dixon."

"So what do you want to do?"

"You aren't going to like it, but you should stay here and let me handle it. I don't think they'll be very talkative if someone of your skin color showed up—let alone the guy who nearly beat the shit out of one of their members while ripping a chunk of his car off."

"And you think you can get them to talk?"

"I'm white and ain't Catholic—isn't that enough for guys like this?"

"So what am I supposed to do? Just stay in Portland and get drunk?"

"Keep an eye on Nichols's place in case anyone else shows up. That was your plan originally, right? And look—you've already had me and Dixon visit the house to prove you're on the right track."

"You're right—I don't like this at all."

"But you know I'm right about it."

"Doesn't mean I have to like it."

"You'll get your second round with Dixon. I promise."

CHAPTER 7

IT TOOK A LITTLE MORE FINA- gling but I was finally able to convince Anderson to let me borrow his car for the trip to Detroit, while he stayed in Portland watching the house. The hour or so it took to get out to the address took me to an entirely different looking state than I always thought Oregon would be. While Portland was the happening city that attracted people from all over the country, the rest of the state was more like the forgotten western wastelands—more like NASCAR country than the thriving liberalness I had driven away from. The kind of place you'd expect a group like the Nordic Hammers to take refuge. Or be birthed from. Probably both.

It took me a couple of wrong turns before I finally was able to find the right barely paved road going up into the mountains. I came upon a dingy cabin that had all the appeal of a mobile home—just without the wheels. A dilapidated porch lined the front of the house that was painted in a disgustingly dirty white—except where the weather had chipped away the original coat. At the end of the deck was a late-model Oldsmobile Cutlass missing a bumper. I drove farther down the road and ditched my car in a pullout by the woods, and then hoofed it on foot back to the house. Knowing these were the kind of guys who showed off their love for weaponry I decided it was best to try and take them by surprise. Walking up and announcing myself would have likely gotten me a "git off my property," or some kind of angry uneducated drawl like that. But if I was to jump in by surprise they'd want to know why I was there, and that would help me start a conversation. Once we had a conversation I could get the information I was looking for. Plus, if it came down to it, my resume of left hooks to Klansmen would do me well against a scrub like Dixon.

The silence of the country put me off a little, as I'd expected someone to be home with the Cutlass sitting outside. Creeping up to the house, I peeked around a few windows without seeing or hearing anyone. Taking my chances, I found the front lock to be a breeze to pick with a credit card, and walked in. I was sure I was alone—so it was a shock to hear a shotgun cock and a voice call out sternly.

"Put your hands up and no quick movements."

I did as I was told and put my hands up. Out of the corner of my eye I saw an older man in his mid-fifties. He had a double-barreled shotgun pointed right at my chest, and a face that told me he was ready to use it without hesitation.

"You have the right to remain silent."

"What the fuck?" was all I could get out.

"Anything you say can and will be used against you in a court of law."

"What the hell is this? Who the hell are you?"

The old man kept one hand on the shotgun, and pulled out a star from around his neck. It read United States Marshal.

"That's who the hell I am. Now turn around slowly. To be honest I'd be glad to have an excuse to put every bit of this buckshot into your liver with no witnesses around. Don't give me a justifiable opportunity."

I did as he asked and slowly turned to face him with my hands still raised. When we finally made eye contact the tension in his face collapsed into a look of pure disappointment.

"Shit," he muttered and pointed the gun to the floor. "You ain't Ricker."

"Who the hell is Ricker?"

"Don't give me that shit. Where is he?"

"I'm telling you, I don't know who Ricker is."

"Then what are you doing in this house?"

"I could ask you the same thing."

"I've got a star and a gun. What do you think I'm doing here? Now you're going to lead me to where he is or I'll take you down for aiding and abetting."

"I told you, I don't know any Ricker. Shit, I must have walked into the wrong house."

"I watched you pick the lock."

"If this is Ricker's place, and I'm supposed to know Ricker, do you think I'd be picking the lock to get in here?"

That gave the marshal a moment of pause. "Then what are you doing breaking into someone's home?"

"I'm looking for Dixon."

"What do you want with that scrub?"

"So you know Dixon? That makes me think I'm in the right place."

"Why would you be going around trying to break into Dixon's place? What are you—another lousy bounty hunter?"

If that was the lifeline he was going to give me, then I was gladly going to take it. "So? What of it?"

The marshal took another moment to think it over before putting the gun on the coffee table nearby and sitting down on a ratty brown cloth couch that had probably been dumped on the side of the road on a number of occasions. "Fucking bounty hunters," he mumbled again. "What are you doing in Oregon? There's no private bail system in the state. We don't need your kind around here."

"I'm in from Texas." I didn't know shit about being a bounty hunter, but if there's any state that would rely on something like that, it would be the Lone Star State. It seemed as good an answer as any.

"When the hell was Dixon ever in Texas to jump bail?"

"Five years ago." I had done the same thing with Ms. Burkhart—if you sound like you know the answer, you're more than likely to get away with it.

Plus, this time I knew the airport carpet was green if asked.

"Let me see your papers," the marshal replied. "I showed you the star, let's call it professional courtesy."

"I don't have them on me."

"Now isn't that convenient?"

"Look, I don't know how you guys out here in Oregon run law enforcement, but only a rookie would bring papers with him on the job. Dixon is a dangerous criminal on the run—I'm not going to walk up with papers, hoping he comes nice and quietly. What's he gonna say? Oh yes, that's me—I guess the paper can't be wrong. Take me away to Texas. Hell no. I'm going to sneak in here and get the drop on him before he even knows what's going on. I'll give him the papers later."

"That's how you do things in Texas?"

"Coming from a state without a private bail system, you shouldn't be running your mouth on how things are supposed to get done in Texas."

That bit of force finally cracked the marshal. He let out a laugh. "All right, Mr. Texas bounty hunter. Do I get a name besides that?"

"Thorne."

"Marshal Palmer," he said, reaching out to shake my hand. "Now tell me, Mr. Thorne, you said your plan was to get the drop on Dixon and take him away without much of a fuss. So what are you going to do when he shows up with a gang of his Hammer brothers?"

"Tell them I'm only here for Dixon, but if any of them want to join him I'd gladly take the whole lot of them in—and since I'm not a cop I don't mind shutting them up with my fists first."

"You look like you could get a couple of good hooks in. You a fighter?"

"Former. Had a run in the Golden Gloves, but nothing past that."

"Then tell me, Mr. Thorne—what are you going to do when they all show up with AR-15s in their hands? What good is your right hook against that?"

"Left hook," I corrected him.

"Shit, no one likes a southpaw."

"Bounty hunters aren't trying to be liked."

"True, that. Still—lefty or righty, you're going up against a bunch of guys with guns."

"Not these guys."

"What do you mean?"

"I'm only on his case again after five years because this dipshit starts posing for pictures with his group. There's a bunch of them online, each with ten to fifteen guys. But they've only got one assault rifle each time—like they're passing it around to pretend they've all got one. If this group was coming in after me all loaded up, they'd be posing with a lot more weaponry."

"What about handguns?"

I thought back to what Anderson had said about how nervous Dixon had been, holding the gun to him during their encounter outside Nichols's place. "Dixon don't know how to use a handgun when the pressure's on. I doubt the rest of them do."

"Well shit, Mr. Thorne, I'll give you credit—you've certainly done your homework. These Nordic

Hammer guys are lacking firepower. I gave this place a run-through before I came into the house myself. Though the group likes to show off their gun online, and though they're out in the middle of nowhere, they ain't left many signs of shooting around here. Oh, a couple of bullet casings, and a dented can or two, but nothing a group like this does to practice and let off steam."

"You're an expert on groups like this?"

"I've hunted down my share of white supremacists. Bunch of stubborn, uneducated trash—each group thinking all they have to do is commit one act of violence that'll start a race war and turn them into heroes. Really they're just a bunch of drug addicts with shitty tattoos watching too much TV in some kind of trailer home in East Bumblefuck, Any State."

"So then what's there to worry about?"

"For someone who seems to have done his homework with their Instagram account—yeah, I've seem those pictures too—you haven't asked me the obvious question."

"Enlighten me," I asked, sarcastically.

"You haven't asked me about Ricker."

"All right, I'll let you have your moment. Who's Ricker?"

"Ricker ain't someone to be messed with. He's not like the rest of these dipshit Hammers—he's a specialist from Idaho."

"A white supremacist specialist? Does he have that printed on his business cards?"

"He's not listed in the yellow pages, if that's

what you're asking. Still, he's a dangerous guy. One of the few in their movement with a brain. You ever see that movie Pulp Fiction?"

"Who hasn't?"

"He's like Harvey Keitel's character."

"The Wolf?"

"That's the one. Ricker floats from group to group, fixing problems, thinking he is getting them ready for the moment the race war finally starts—when some dipshit kills one guy and the whole country turns to a civil war. At least that's the thinking of a bunch of dipshits like them."

"So he gets rid of bodies and cleans out bloody cars when called?"

"Not exactly. More like he helps get groups funded with the drug trade. Maybe telling them how to pull prospective recruits their way. Helping them work the firearm black market to pull in more than just one AR-15 for their group shots."

"Our boys are in the heroin trade?"

"Nah, that's way too high-class for them. They're straight-up meth-heads. I like to think they are personally responsible for why you can't even get Sudafed in this state without a prescription."

"And Ricker is now leading this flock of losers known as the Hammers?"

"Only until I get my shotgun pointed at him."

"If he's as dangerous as you say, why the hell are you sneaking into this place by yourself?"

"I know you're new to Oregon, but do you really think law enforcement would send anyone out to the middle of nowhere? The Portland police department is so short on bodies they made a rule to only use thirty-one officers for any one event. State cops help out at times, in the one city where most of the population lives. Last thing they want is to loan anyone out on a goose chase for an Idaho guy who isn't officially wanted."

"If he isn't officially wanted, what's a marshal doing after him?"

"He's done enough to warrant it. No one will question me when I bring him in. Not even if there's any kind of buckshot in him."

"Sounds personal."

"He's fucking up my beautiful country. Hell yeah, it's personal."

"How long have you been here waiting for him?"

"You're the only movement I've had in the last five hours."

Knowing what side of the law I normally fall on, I decided the last thing I wanted to do was wait around with any kind of law enforcer, marshal or otherwise. "Well, I'm not waiting that long. Let me know if anything happens."

He reached into his pocket and pulled out a worn white business card with a marshal's star on the left side and the name Palmer in raised black lettering on the right. "How will I get in touch with you?"

"I'll give you a call," I snapped back as I turned toward the door to leave. "Last thing I want is any kind of Oregon rules getting in the way of some Texas judgment." I closed the door and walked out before he had a chance to answer.

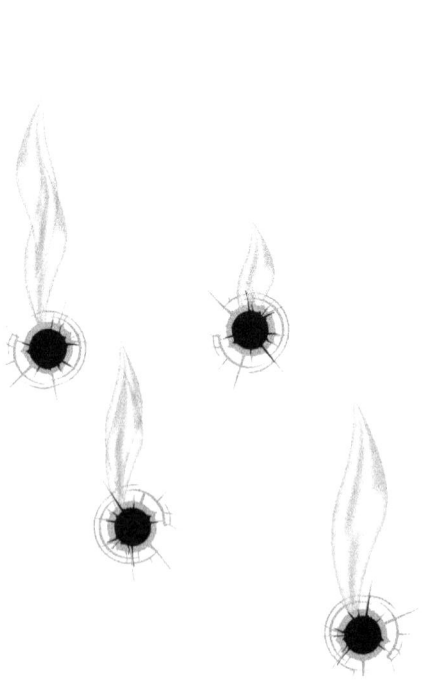

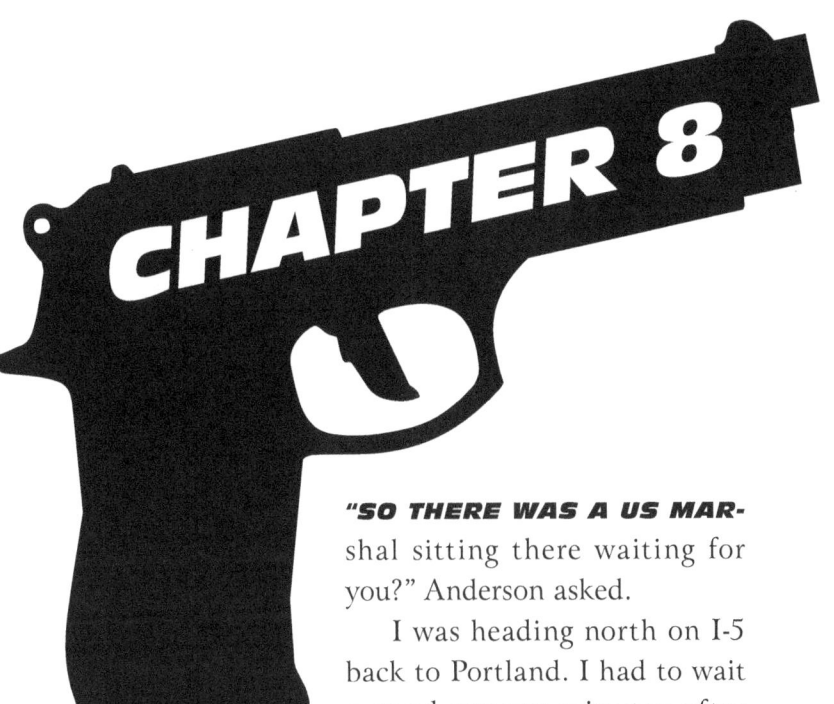

CHAPTER 8

"SO THERE WAS A US MAR- shal sitting there waiting for you?" Anderson asked.

I was heading north on I-5 back to Portland. I had to wait a good twenty minutes after leaving the cabin in Detroit before I could get signal service to call Dynamite and give him the update. "Nah, he wasn't waiting for me."

"Who was he waiting for then?"

"Ricker."

"Who the hell's Ricker? I thought you were going to meet Dixon."

"Yeah. Dixon was a no-show."

"Because there was a marshal at the place, waiting?"

"I get the feeling they were just on different schedules. In fact the marshal is probably still there."

"But he's not waiting for Dixon."

"I was there for Dixon, he was there for Ricker."

"And will you tell me who Ricker is?"

"My guess is he's our guy who killed Finn."

"How do you figure that?"

"The marshal pretty much laid it out that the Hammers we're dealing with are closer to being the Keystone Cops of racial hatred. He picked up what you were saying—that they looked like they couldn't even arm themselves properly. But this Ricker guy is a specialist who's come to town to whip the troops into shape."

"And you think Ricker killed Finn but sent his lackey Dixon to do Nichols?"

"You said yourself that Dixon was pure amateur in trying to break in. But Finn was done right—sneak up to him and put two in his chest without him even knowing it. A guy who double-times both Hartford and Providence—while running guns and dealing with the Mexican cartel—isn't easy to sneak up on. No way was that Dixon or any of his Hammer boys. But if Ricker is as good as the marshal says, then he'd fit that profile."

"That still doesn't answer why these guys bumped off Finn and went after Nichols next."

"I know, but it's the best we've got so far."

"So what are we going to do now?"

"You stay put, keeping an eye on Nichols's house, just in case. I'm going to make a stop at our favorite Unity Coalition office and see what I can scare up. The woman running a 'we are the world kumbaya peace and love' group has her top donor likely gunned down by a white supremacist group. That certainly will have the press running to her. Then someone will look at her books and see that she's been laundering drug money and the jig will be up."

"You think it's good enough to blackmail her for the cash?"

"No, but it's better than nothing. Maybe light a fire under her ass and see where it takes us. I'll stop by the house afterwards."

"And bring that car back too. Been standing out here all day without a chance to get a burger or something."

Fighting the tradition of awful Portland traffic, it took me another solid hour to get back into the city and make a stop at the small office of the Portland Unity Coalition. Ms. Burkhart was alone and sat behind her desk almost as if she had never bothered to leave since the last time I paid a visit. Since we were old pals by now I figured there was no need to knock, and allowed myself into her office.

"Ms. Burkhart, what a pleasure to see you again."

I gave her credit for not showing surprise at my reappearance, considering how contentious our last meeting was. She kept her hands on her lap as innocently as possible while putting all kinds of violence in her stare. "Mr. Williams," she muttered sarcastically. "To what do I owe this pleasure?"

I took the seat across from her with my charming grin. "An old friend can't just stop by and say hello?"

"That only applies to friends I am happy to see." Ice-cold bitch.

"Friends like Mr. Finn?"

"Can you not leave the poor man alone and let his soul be at peace?"

I made what I thought was the sign of the cross, passing my hand over my head, chest, and shoulders. "My apologies. I do not wish to besmirch dearly departed Mr. Finn's spotless reputation. No—today I actually come to ask you about some other friends of yours. A Mr. Tyler Dixon, perhaps?"

She took a moment to calculate her next words, not allowing me any kind of read on her. "Am I supposed to know who Tyler Dixon is?"

"Well, he is affiliated with a certain group of deplorables that I feel a charity like the Portland Unity Coalition would be interested in."

"And what group is that?"

"Come now, you must know of the Nordic Hammers."

"Nordic Hammers? Did you get that off the marquee over at the Hawthorne Theater? Why, yes—I think they're opening for the Mutant Squirrels on Saturday."

"So the name Ricker doesn't mean anything to you either?"

"Ricker? Is he like a Brazilian soccer star with just one name? Or a pop star, like Madonna?"

"Ha-ha, that's a good one." I poured on the mock laughter. "I thought you'd be more interested in the guy most likely responsible for the murder of your biggest donor."

"Where are you getting that information? More of your shoddy newspaper investigations?"

"Let's just say a little birdie told me. But then I

get to the idea that here's a woman running a group that prides itself on unity—and yet the man most likely running dirty money through it ends up dead at the hands of a known white supremacist who is connected to a local white power group—all conveniently located in the free and open and Bernie Sanders-loving town of Portland. Now that seems like a bit of a coincidence doesn't it?"

She kept up her bitch face. I kept up my charming grin. We made a lovely pair. "I would certainly say so," she finally replied.

"See, in my years of experience I've come to realize just how pathetic 'coincidence' is as a word. It's really just a lazy copout to doing the real work and finding out the truth of how the events are connected. Oh sure, coincidences happen in movies all the time, to get people to believe that they're real—but this ain't Hollywood. You know more than you let on."

"Is that so?" She paused again. "So let me get this straight. You think I run a unity coalition and hired a known white supremacist to kill my biggest donor in order to hide the fact that he was laundering money through my group? Is that your idea?"

"Let me spin the future for you a different way. I feel like the press would love a story where a big-time donor to a group like yours ends up dead at the hands of someone like Ricker. They'd just eat that up. Then they'd start digging into Finn's finances and discover that he's had his hands in gun running and heroin dealing and then passed the rewards to a group run by seemingly just one person, considering the lack of staff you seem to always have when I make my visits. That isn't going to look good for you, especially as a woman with so much to hide."

"How dare you! You come into my office for a second time and start throwing mud on me, my donors, and our mission."

"I believe the last time I paid you a visit you said you would call the cops on me if I ever came back. Well, here I am and you haven't reached for the phone yet. Seems like getting the authorities involved is the last thing you want. Plus there's the .25 millimeter you've got in your hands behind the desk. An odd choice for someone running a small charity organization."

Since I called her out on it, she pulled the gun out and held it on the desk while still aiming it at me. "Maybe I have this just for when you stopped by again."

"If that was the case you would have waved it in front of me already, to try and scare me off."

"Then what's your point in being here?"

"A proposition. As of right now I am the only one who knows who killed Pete Finn—well, myself and my partner, but that's it. Now I'm not the police or anything even remotely close to that. But I'm a man who's looking for the tens of thousands of dollars that Pete stole from my employer. Money we haven't found yet—which means it's likely hidden in your books."

"So that's what this is about? Blackmail?"

"If you want to think of it like that."

"That's the stupidest thing I've ever heard."

"If you want to think of it like that. Then again,

it means you'll have to risk a juicy story leaking out to the press and someone going through your books and finding something you don't want them to."

"I can live with that."

"And what happens when Ricker comes looking for you?"

"What makes you say that'd happen?"

"You've got the gun already prepared for when he does. He's already killed the dearly departed Mr. Finn and sent his goons to wipe out Finn's associate. You clearly know that it's only a matter of time, and that you're next on the list. I drop a hint to the press and that'll make him come after you faster. So really it's up to you how you want to play this."

"And you'll just let this Ricker come after me?"

"Sorry, I'm only getting paid to find the money Pete owes my employer. I'm not in the bodyguarding business. At least you look like you know how to hold a .25. I'll give you about a ten percent chance against Ricker."

I stood up with a grin and gave her a wink. "Have a good night, Ms. Burkhart," I said as I left.

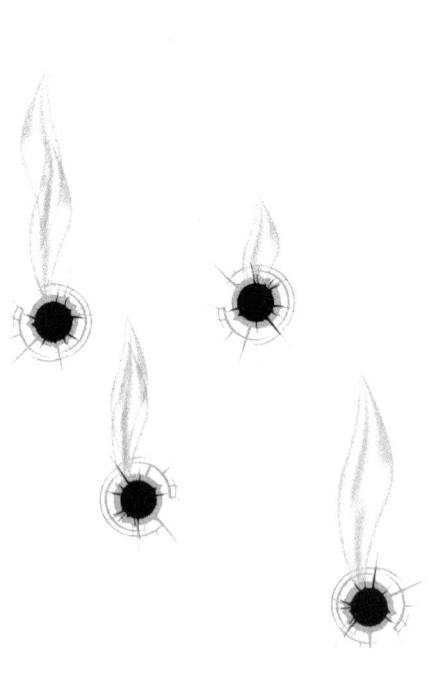

CHAPTER 9

AFTER FINISHING WITH MS. Burkhart I got into Anderson's car and gave him a call to update him on my progress with the head of the coalition, but after four rings it automatically cut off. It did the same thing the next three times I tried calling him. I jumped on 84 to I-5 and made my way to the dingy pothead's house in the north quadrant. Instead of the quiet neighborhood, I found three police cars, an EMT truck, and enough caution tape to stretch back to Hartford.

Anyone driving by a crime scene slowly the first time just looks like a normal rubbernecker trying to figure out what gruesome event happened, so when they see it on the six o'clock news they can brag to their spouse that they had been there. But drive by a second time and usually someone on the police team takes notice, figuring you're either a rookie reporter who is too afraid to step up to a police officer, or someone connected to the incident. Since my attempt at pretending to be the press didn't go so well with Ms. Burkhart, I figured I'd get figured out easily for being the latter category. In that situation it's better to just own up to it and confront the cops directly. That way you turn into a sympathetic family member rather than a skeevy ex-boxer in a crappy car driving by a pothead's house.

I parked the car as close as I could and hurried up to the caution tape where a cop stepped in my way.

"What the hell is going on here?" I asked.

"Whoa, whoa—slow down, there."

"No—you slow down. Jimmy asked me to check in on his house while he was away, and I stop by and there's all these cops around. What the hell am I supposed to tell him?"

"You know Mr. Nichols?"

"Yeah, I'm the guy who's been telling him he needed to fix that front door for a while. It's so flimsy anyone who wanted to rob him could just kick it in easily. That's not what happened here, is it?"

"No, nothing happened inside the house. You wouldn't happen to know where we could find Mr. Nichols, do you?"

"He's in Colorado for the week—at least that's what he told me." If I couldn't find where he had flown off to, I doubt the cops could. No harm in dropping the lie that made me fit the profile of a house sitter.

The cop considered this for a second, but clearly bought into what I was saying. "Was anyone else supposed to be looking after his house with you?"

"Why? What's this all about? Especially if no one went into the house like you're saying."

The cop looked around nervously, first back at the crime scene and then toward what I could only guess was a detective higher up the food chain. "Well, shit—it's going to be lighting up Twitter soon anyway, so I might as well tell you. There was a guy got beaten up really bad behind the house."

I tried putting on my most sympathetic face but don't think I pulled it off. "Has there been a rash of these things lately? You said it would be all over Twitter."

"It was a black man. He's in real bad shape. Shit, they worked him over good, from head to toe."

"A black man? Do you know his name?"

"Uh—that I can't remember. I heard a powder keg or a bomb or—"

"Dynamite?"

"Yeah that's it! You know him?"

"Yeah I know him. Where is he?"

"Emmanuel Hospital. Hey wait, we need to take down your information in case we need to get in touch with you ..."

I didn't give the cop a chance to stop me. I jumped back in the car and booked it as fast as I could over to Emmanuel. I didn't even concentrate on the drive. I couldn't remember a single stop light or the color of a single car I passed—normally the details I pride myself in picking out of everyday life to help me in the loan-shark business. All I could see was Dynamite in the middle of the ring the first time he went clobbering me with that right hand. He beat the shit out of me that night but I never went down. It was a warrior's mentality from both of us in that bout—the kinship of those who have gone through the ropes and respected the sweet science.

So many boxers are dirt-poor and from the streets, like myself and Anderson. We start without money, we become boxers, we get punched in the head, and we end up without money. But at least we were trying to do something about it. You don't know the story of everyone you fight, but for better or worse the moment you get into that ring and put on those gloves you're in the fraternity of the desperate. You'll never be able to connect with someone more than when they are connecting right hooks to your jaw. My employer never understood it—neither did Anderson's mob bosses in Providence. But right now they were 3,000 miles away. Here in Portland there was only me and my fraternity brother—and anyone who messed with him was going to find out just how strong that ring bond is.

I didn't remember where I parked, but I did find the front desk of the emergency room and demanded to know where Dynamite was. The nurse kept her cool. I'm sure she gets riled-up family members asking where loved ones are at least three times a day. I was nothing but old hat to her. About half an hour after the nurse told me to sit and wait, she finally came over, saying that I could go in and see Mr. Anderson.

Outside his room was a police officer, making sure no one went in or out without proper authorization. I understood why the cop at Nichols's place didn't chase me down—he knew where I would be going.

"Who's this?" the guard asked.

"This is Mr. Thorne," the nurse said, matter-of-factly.

"He's Thorne?"

"Yeah I am," I said. "What of it?"

"The guy in there's been asking for you. Only thing we've been able to get out of him so far. He's messed up really good. Just wanted to give you the warning."

I gave the guard a mean glare and then walked in behind the nurse. The room was annoyingly bright, as you'd expect from a hospital. Anderson was on the bed in the middle of it, hooked up to wires and tubes that led to slowly beeping machines. An oxygen tube went to his nose and an IV ran from a plastic bag to his right arm. I remember all the pain he would dish out with that right arm, and now it was desperately taking all the painkillers it could get. His face was bandaged with gauze that couldn't hide the bruising and swelling exploding on his features. His left leg was elevated and in a tight brace, under even more wrappings that hid the damage to his knee. I'd seen plenty of fighters beaten up past recognition, but looking at Dynamite now made me more depressed than ever.

Sensing someone else was in the room, Anderson wiggled slightly, and I caught a glimpse of him eyeing me. He tried to say something to the nurse but could only get out a whisper.

"What was that?" she asked.

He tried again, without any luck. I decided to step in.

"Could I speak with him alone?" I asked.

Hearing that, Dynamite slowly nodded. I added: "I promise not to mess with any of the medical hookups you have here."

The nurse gave us a stern look to make sure I stayed on my best behavior. "I don't know how the officer would feel about that but I'll give you five minutes. I know it's hard on friends and family for people in the ICU. Just make sure you grab a doctor if alarms start to ring in here."

"I will," I said. "Thank you for understanding." I tried my smile again as I watched her walk out and close the door.

I turned to Anderson. "What the hell happened, man? You're a mess."

"No shit," he mumbled. At least that's what I thought I heard him say. His voice was so quiet and shaky from the mixture of the beating and the painkillers that it seemed to be a struggle for him just to form words. Between the two of us, I always thought I was the tougher one, especially for taking the hammering he had given me in the semifinals. Looking at him now, I knew that wasn't the case.

"You get hit by a car or something?"

"Fucking Hammers."

"The Hammers?"

"They were waiting for me."

"What do you mean, waiting for you?"

"They were at the house, watching me watch the house. You said they weren't at Dixon's place. They were waiting at Nichols's place."

"How do you know it was them?"

"I recognized some of them from the pictures. Dixon was there."

"What makes you say they were waiting for you?"

"They said so. They took pleasure in beating me, saying it was payback time."

"Just for that little scrap with Dixon?"

"I don't know, but there were a bunch of them. Four or five, I guess. They jumped me from behind before I even knew what was going on. I gave out a couple of good shots, but then the man giving orders got me across the knee with a crowbar. Shit, man … it's … it's busted for good."

"Don't say that," I said. "You've been busted up before. You'll be back in the ring in a few months."

"I hear the doctors. They think I'm totally out of it, but I hear things. They don't think I'll ever walk correctly again."

"What do some lousy doctors know?"

Even if he wasn't hooked up to all the machines, he wouldn't be able to move more than an inch on his own. Tears started falling down his cheeks at the thought of being confined to a bed for the rest of his life. There's no pain more painful than that which destroys the toughest of us.

"I know it's hard, but tell me all you can remember. I'm going to get those fucking Hammers."

"I don't remember much besides the kicks and the crowbar. It's all just dark and red. But I can still hear the guy calling the shots with his high-pitched voice. Asking me how I liked the beating and calling me every kind of racial slur imaginable."

"High-pitched?" I asked, but I already knew the

answer to the question in my mind. It had to be Ricker. The marshal knew he was hanging around the Hammers today, and there was no chance they could pull off something like this without his help. Alone they couldn't even break into a house—but with Ricker they could organize themselves, jump a mafia muscle man, and beat an ex-boxer nearly to death.

"Why didn't they kill me?" Anderson asked painfully.

"You're too damn tough."

"They shot Pete no problem, and were going after Nichols. Why not kill me?"

"Don't you worry about that." I patted the side of his hand to let him know I was still there for him. Through a slight window in the door I could see the guard about to turn the handle and enter. I guess the nurse hadn't been able to buy us the full five minutes. But it had been enough. "I'm going to get those fuckers."

I beat the guard to the punch and started to head out of the room, but not before asking him as we crossed paths by the door, "Do you have any idea who would do such a thing?"

"No clue so far," the guard replied. "I'm not on the case, just standing guard. But when he was brought in I overheard them saying they're afraid it was just a random attack. Last thing this town needs is a crew going around beating up random civilians like that—especially someone who's a minority."

I nodded.

"You wouldn't know anything about this, would

you?" the guard asked. "Something to help us move the case forward?"

"Not a clue. Anderson said he got jumped from behind, but never saw who it was."

"That's a shame. Will be hard to track these guys down, then."

"Let's hope they get what's coming to them," I said, and headed toward the exit. The car was in the garage and had enough gas to get to Detroit.

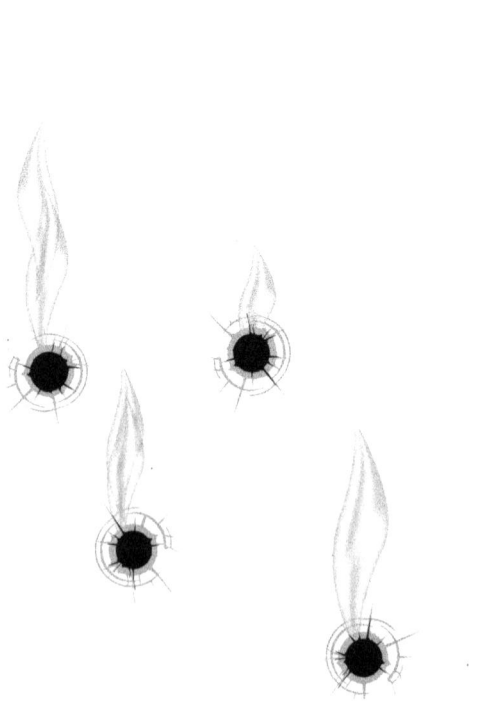

CHAPTER 10

SOME FIGHTERS IN THE lower ranks are able to get their names up the ladder based entirely on blood wrath. When they get in the ring they turn into adrenaline-fueled monsters, and don't even remember where they are. They just start throwing haymakers at every turn and only need one to connect for them to knock their opponent out for the count. Club promoters love those guys because the paying customer rarely has to wait for a second round to see a vicious knockout.

The only problem with these fighters is that when they start playing the bigger clubs they come up against boxers with more between their ears than just targets. The latter keep the red from their vision and know how to dance away from the blood-wrath guys with quick jabs here and there while waiting for their chance. One wild missed hook leaves the opponent exposed and suddenly the red vision turns to black when they're on their back on the canvas with the ref counting to ten. You never see a blood-wrath guy make it big, but they'll spend the rest of their lives on the stoop telling anyone who will listen that they could have made it, and threatening to knock out the lights of anyone who brings up the fact that they got themselves cleaned out in the second round by a smarter boxer.

Never being the strongest puncher in the division, I learned to be a thinker in the ring, and put away enough of those adrenaline junkies to make it all the way to the semifinals. Keeping my composure in the ring was my biggest weapon. At least that's what I kept telling myself as I pulled up to Dixon's trailer. I could just barge in there and beat the shit out of anyone I saw, but that would only have gotten me a hospital bed next to Anderson. I needed to take this to the second round.

By now the place was nearly pitch-black, with a nearly new moon offering little help. I turned off the headlights and slowly inched the car closer, trying not to rev the engine. I found the same empty spot I had ditched the car in before, and walked through the woods to get a better look at the place. Lights inside the trailer seemed extra-bright, as they were the only illumination for miles. Inside, I could hear yelling, drinking, and celebrating over the sound of awful skinhead punk rock that would make Johnny Rotten cringe.

With my targets in the light, I kept my distance in the woods. After an hour of keeping tabs on the place I was able to pick out the three men inside as Dixon and two of his Nordic Hammer brothers, who I recognized from the pictures. My guess at what they were celebrating made me even more irritated, but I had to keep my cool.

Two hours later the punk music was still going strong but the other sounds of merriment had died down. No more beer and yelling. I got up closer to the trailer and peeked in the windows. The other two Hammers were passed out—one sprawled across the sofa, the other on a ripped-up recliner with a half-empty Rainier still clutched in his hand. Dixon was stumbling around but still on his feet. He grabbed a pack of smokes from a table and walked outside.

He made sure to close the door quietly so he wouldn't disturb the passed-out guests—as if they would have been able to hear the door over the blaring music. He lit a cigarette and took a deep sigh. Being a nice guy, I let him have a few puffs. He never saw me hiding in the shadows. What he did see was my left hook hitting him square on the jaw. That dropped him instantly. I might not have been the strongest in the division, but Dixon was a bantamweight at best. One hook was all I needed for the job.

Before Dixon could get a cry of pain out I started in with kicks to his stomach, robbing him of his breath. While he was trying to regain his breath, I grabbed his collar, pulling him up to a sitting position, and hitting him again with a left. He needed to be taught a lesson. While he sobbed on the ground, I frisked him quickly, but didn't find any weapons. Still wary of the duo passed out inside, I picked Dixon up by the collar again, but this time got him to his feet, and forced him to walk into the dark woods.

"Please ... please stop ..." he begged.

"Oh, stop? Stop?" I threw another left but this time right into his gut, sending him back down to the canvas. Even in the dim light I could see he was spitting up blood. "You don't mind dishing out the punishment but you're afraid to take it?"

"What ... what are you talking about? Please ... stop ..."

"I'm talking about you and your fucking Hammers."

"I didn't do anything ..."

"You didn't? You didn't joy-ride into Portland today and beat someone nearly to death?"

"We didn't do anything. You can't arrest me."

"Do I look like a fucking cop?"

"No ..."

"Damn straight. A cop would have had you in cuffs already. But me? Hell, I can keep whupping up on you all I want. Now, were you in Portland today or do I need to start breaking ribs with some more lefts?"

"Stop! Please ... yes ... yes ... we were in Portland today."

"And beating on someone?"

"Yes ... yes ... that bodyguard."

"Bodyguard?"

"The guy Nichols hired."

"What guy?"

"The black guy."

"What makes you think he was a bodyguard?"

"I don't know, man ..."

I feinted like I was about to slug him again when he quickly relented. "Okay ... okay ... He was there the other night. I went to take care of Nichols and that black guy was there. He jumped me from behind like he was watching and waiting for me."

"Why were you going to Nichols's that night?"

"Just to talk to him."

"Bullshit. The story I heard is you were trying to break in to kill him with a .35. Yeah, I know more than you think I do, so don't get on with your lying and think you're fucking Einstein."

"Okay ... I had the gun but I didn't want to kill him if I didn't have to. I just wanted to find the money."

"What money?"

"Nichols is fucking loaded."

"That guy? In that crappy house with the messed-up front door? All he had was a piece-of-crap TV and a couple of bongs."

"He's got the cash stashed in there somewhere. How do you think he got enough to pay for a bodyguard like that? An out-of-town guy too."

"And where did Nichols get all this cash?"

"From that Finn guy."

"How do you know that?"

"It was all Ricker's idea."

"Why are you trying to pass the buck onto someone else?"

"No ... no ... please don't. It was Ricker! He told me to hit up Nichols."

"To take out a drug rival?" I asked.

"Drug rival?" Dixon seemed genuinely confused.

"I know about you rednecks running meth across the state."

"Nichols was dealing meth too?"

"Isn't that why you guys had beef with him—over drug turf?"

"Hell, no."

"Then why did Ricker want to take out Nichols?"

"Nichols is a gunrunner."

"A gunrunner? That guy? He's stoned out of his mind twenty-four seven. You can't run guns like that."

"He and that Finn guy were in on it together. They used to rip us off every time we tried to get some guns ourselves. I don't know how they did it, but they kept screwing up our orders."

"Your orders? Like you calling up Amazon and asking for some AKs?"

"I don't know how—that was all Chester's doing." He nodded toward the trailer, suggesting Chester was one of those passed out inside. "He said he knew a couple of guys but every time we tried to get our hands on anything big this Finn guy beat us to the punch and outbid us."

"Why didn't you just get Ricker to get you some guns?"

"Ricker only just got here a few weeks ago. He was up in Idaho or something for a while and just jumped into the group."

"You just let him in the Hammers?"

"Hell, yeah. He got us an automatic rifle quickly and started telling us what we should be doing with it—like hitting up some of the black neighborhoods infecting the city. He said the guys in Idaho sent him to start cleaning the place up for what was coming next."

"And what is coming next?"

"I don't know, man ... please ... please don't hit me again!"

"What's next?"

"I don't know! But Ricker's got some kind of plan. I seen him texting back and forth with some guys in Idaho."

"And Ricker killed Finn?"

"Shit ... you know about that?"

"I couldn't picture you dumb shits being able to do the deed yourself. If he already killed Finn, then why send you after Nichols?"

"There wasn't any money at Finn's place. That means it all had to be at Nichols's. A guy who's running guns like that has to deal in cash to avoid the cops. Look at me, man—I'm living in a fucking trailer in the middle of nowhere. I need that money. I need to get me a place back in the city. So I volunteered. Ricker just wanted Nichols dead and didn't care about anything that happened afterwards."

"So you figured you could kill Nichols and look around the house, take the money yourself, and then say you never found it?"

"Look at what happens when these guys come over—they bust my place up all the time. I deserve that money."

"If Nichols had all this money there, then why didn't the whole group go back today to look for the cash?"

"I don't think Ricker knew about the money—or he at least he didn't care about it."

"Then why go to Nichols's?"

"He wanted the bodyguard."

"For what?"

"Shit ... he ... he went off on me when I came back beaten up and without the gun from when I went to bump Nichols off. But when I told him about the black bodyguard he completely changed and started talking about how we have a target to get things in motion."

"Why not just kill him?"

"Ricker said specifically not to. Something about how random killings have never started the war so it was time to try something else. He said, 'Kill a man and he becomes a statistic. But leave him disfigured and he'll make actual news. Our Aryan brothers will see the work we're doing in Portland and join us.'"

I thought back to my dealings with the Klan in Connecticut and how the mindset seemed the same. Just as stupid, and in their own minds extremely strategic, like they were going to change the world with one action. "You really ready to start a race war?"

Dixon hesitated. "No ... no, not really. Look, I hate them ni—"

I pulled back to throw another punch before he caught himself.

"I mean I hate them, er ... African Americans, just like anybody else. You ever go over to Eightieth Street? See them sittin' in front of the 7-Eleven, blaring that awful rap shit and talking trash in the middle of the day. They ain't doing nothin' for the city except making it dirtier, louder, and grosser."

I looked back to the trailer and then back to Dixon. "So what do you call the shit punk music you've got blaring in the trailer? I take it you weren't doing much besides talking trash in the middle of the day yourself."

"Portland is for us whites. Always has been and always will be. I don't want to start no race war, man—I just want my city back for the right people."

"And your plan to do that was to kill a white guy named Finn and then go after another white guy named Nichols?"

"I told you—that was all Ricker's doing. He said it was the first step."

"And the bodyguard was next?"

For the first time Dixon let out a slight laugh, showing he was regaining his confidence. "I'm not up for a full war, but I can't say I didn't enjoy beating the shit out of that guy. Whupping up on any darkie is always a good time."

I threw another left hook square into his stomach, sending him back down to the ground gasping for breath. "That darkie wasn't a bodyguard. You beat up a good friend of mine who is the rightful owner of the cash that Nichols has. All we wanted was the money and to get out of everyone's way—but you had to go and make things difficult. Now I've got to go around and personally beat the crap out of every one of you fucking Hammers."

I think Dixon knew what was coming next but there was nothing I was going to let him do about it. He tried to stand up but left himself in a perfect position for a three-punch combo that knocked his lights out for the rest of the night. My corner man would have been impressed with my speed on the jab-jab-hook to the jaw. Dixon would be out of action for quite a while.

I left him on the ground in the woods and made my way to the trailer. The other two were still passed out, and the punk music covered all other noises, allowing me to slip in with ease. The Hammer on the couch was easy to wake up with a couple of shoves. Still groggy, he was an easy target—I hit him with another vicious combo that sent him right back into the dream world. By the time I followed suit with the guy passed out on the recliner, my hands were swelling up. The last thing I did was grab a baseball bat from the corner and put it to good use on the stereo, silencing another skinhead punk song. I was satisfied with my work and drove back to Portland.

Maybe I'd get lucky and find the cash in Nichols's place, which meant I wouldn't have to keep trying to get it out of Ms. Burkhart by blackmail. Then again, nothing is ever that easy.

CHAPTER 11

IT WAS STILL NIGHT WHEN I got back to Portland and scoped out Nichols's place to make sure no one else from the Hammers was keeping tabs on it before breaking in. The place was a mess, with cereal boxes and dirty dishes everywhere. It wasn't messy in a someone-had-rampaged-the-place kind of way, but rather in a guy-with-no-ambitions-living-a-stoner's-life kind of way. Since the place looked like a dump already, I didn't mind tearing it up a bit more. But nothing coughed up any cash. If Nichols had hightailed it out of town after my first visit there was a good chance he took it with him, but I had my doubts. There were no secure places to have stashed that kind of money in the house—if he ever had it to begin with. No safes anywhere in the place—no false boards in the floors, or holes in the wall behind a bookcase. If Nichols was as loaded as Dixon had claimed, then he didn't keep the money in the house. If it wasn't here, and Finn never kept it, then where did the cash from gun running go? At least ten thousand went to the Portland Unity Coalition—but listening to Dixon, and giving Finn's gun running book another look, I knew there was a lot more than that. And that wasn't even counting the heroin operation he was running.

While I was going through the notebooks again I got two phone calls nearly back to back. The first was the employer, reminding me that I was still working on company time and that he was getting angry because I was putting in overtime on this job. I never told him about the Providence angle, figuring the less he knew the better. Plus, he'd shit a brick if he knew I was working with Anderson. In the end, all he cares about is his money—if I show up with it he won't care how I got it. It's not as if he would ever be dealing with Finn again. Ricker had already cleared that up. No need for Hartford to know about Providence, and vice versa.

The second call came from a 503 number I had never seen before, and I ignored it. In my line of work, nothing good ever comes from answering an unknown caller. It was probably a wrong number or someone calling when the burner phone digits belonged to someone else. It happens from time to time. What doesn't happen that often is when the same 503 number calls a second time. And a third. And a fourth—all within ten minutes. Just to get the ringing to stop I decided to answer the fifth call.

"About time, Mr. Thorne—I've been trying

to reach you for a while now. Only twenty more attempts before I was going to give up."

"I'm sorry, but there's no Mr. Thorne here. You must have the wrong number." At least I tried.

The caller didn't acknowledge my comment. "Did you know I did a thorough check of everyone with a bounty hunter's license in the state of the Texas and didn't come up with a single one matching your name? Then I decided to look through the rest of the state's law enforcement departments—and might I add, there's a lot of names and departments in Texas."

Shit. It was the marshal.

"Local law enforcement, state, feds ... even the Rangers are still down there. Although I'm guessing you wouldn't know that, since not a single person I've talked to has ever heard of you."

"I don't need to listen to any of this."

"Well I'd advise you not to hang up, or else I'm going to keep calling and calling to annoy you all day."

"How did you get this number?"

"I'm a federal marshal. How do you think I got it? The same way that I could find your exact location right now if I really wanted to. You aren't as invisible as you'd like to think, Mr. Thorne. But here's the catch—you're not the one I really care about."

"There's someone else who's stolen your heart?"

"I heard about how your date with Dixon went."

"I don't know what you're talking about."

"You don't think I just stopped keeping tabs on the trailer, do you? Game called early on account of rain? I saw you up there last night. It was some nice work. Really loved that three-punch combo at the end."

"If you saw me up there, why didn't you stop me?"

"I told you—you're not the one I'm after. Neither is Dixon, to be honest. I've got enough of a headache trying to track down my man that the last thing I need is to get involved in whatever you and that dumbass white supremacist have cooking up between you."

"Then why call me? Shouldn't you be staking out the place for your man?"

"I think we need to talk."

"Ain't that what we're doing right now?"

"In person."

"So you can arrest me?"

"You know how they say 'Don't mess with Texas?' Well I don't plan on that at all. Arresting you for impersonating a bounty hunter from that state sounds like a lot of paperwork I don't want anything to do with. What I do want to know is if I can trust you in person not to pull a gun to blow me away so you can go back to your ghost status."

"Then what are you suggesting?"

"Head over to Providence Park. There's a bar across the street called the Bullpen. With a Timbers game today, the place will be packed with fans pregaming with copious amounts of cheap beer. The place will be too noisy for eavesdroppers and too many witnesses for you to pull anything.

"And how will I know you won't try to pull anything yourself and bring some of Portland's finest with you?"

"The place will be too crowded with drunkards. And if you're as good with moving in a crowd as you are with using your fists, you won't have anything to worry about, even if I do bring some friends."

I gave it a few moments of thought. I still hated the layout but it seemed to be as solid a deal as I was going to get. After all, if the marshal was able to find my phone number, he could probably use his fancy federal policing agency gadgets to hunt me down, too. Moving straight to a face-to-face talk was the least-worst option.

"Give me a couple of hours."

"I'll see you there at five," he said, stealing the last word and hanging up on me.

Providence Park was built as a track stadium nearly a century ago, and was recently renovated into a state-of-the-art soccer stadium. It is just west of downtown, and on game day parking is a nightmare. I was forced to take the MAX over to the Goose Hollow neighborhood.

In its traditionally untraditional fashion, Portland has a hardcore love affair with its Timbers soccer team. Over 21,000 rabid fans pack the place every game day, and it seemed like they were all squeezed into the Bullpen bar to drink up before kickoff. The scene inside was a deafening buzz of white noise. I arrived an hour early to get the jump on Palmer, but the marshal was already waiting for me at a booth not too far from the entrance, with a tall glass filled with something hoppy.

"I didn't expect you'd show for at least another half an hour," he said, grinning. He seemed proud to be there first.

"How did you convince your bosses to stop keeping tabs on Dixon's place for this long? Or do they know you've abandoned your post?" It was the best comeback I could think of as I sat down across from him. I had the exit about twenty feet behind me, which would make a quick escape difficult. But it also meant I was able to watch most of the bar and keep tabs on any undercovers trying to swoop in on me. That's if I could even tell who was who. With so many soccer fans in jerseys and scarves, and sporting empty pints, it would be easy to blend in.

"I have a feeling Ricker won't be showing up there again anytime soon. It appears someone put a smackdown on his boys. If he's as smart as I think he is, the last place he'd be is somewhere that's now unsafe to the point anyone can just show up and whup on his crew."

"Is he that smart?"

"I'd think so. He's much smarter than you are, at least."

"Is this how you start all of your conversations—by insulting your guests?"

"If you were as smart as I think you are, you'd have hightailed it out of here the second I hung up with you. Yet here you are. That means one of two things: either you're incredibly stupid to be following the orders of a fed, or beating up on Dixon wasn't the endgame of your trip out here."

"How do you know I'm not from here originally?"

"You wouldn't have wasted the time to make up that crap about being from Texas, which gave you an out in case you tipped your hand."

"Maybe I'm actually much smarter than you think Ricker is, and am really three steps ahead of all of you."

"What's the river that flows through the city?"

"The Willamette," I said, proudly.

"Congrats," he said in a mocking tone. "You said Willamette, when anyone from Oregon knows it's the Willamette. Add that to your not hightailing it out of here, and that makes two strikes against you, Mr. Thorne. I hope you have a surprising batting average in the clutch."

"It's better than my scouting report says."

"It had better be." He took another sip of beer. "I hope you know who you're dealing with now that you've left a mark on the Hammers."

"Are you talking about our mysterious friend Ricker? I can handle him."

"Ricker isn't like those bumbling dipshits you put beat up at Dixon's place. They're a bunch of uneducated wannabes who can't shoot and spend their days talking up how tough they are to anyone against the white race, but then drink and smoke so much they never leave the couch to actually do anything about it."

"If they never leave the couch, then where were they when we had our first rendezvous?" I knew damn well where they were, but I wasn't going to give away any information to a marshal unless he showed he already knew it. So far he didn't seem to know I had a hospitalized partner from Providence and I wanted to keep it that way.

"I don't think you're grasping the full danger of what Ricker can do."

"These guys aren't wearing any hoods but I've dealt with the Klan before in a different part of the country. All talk blaming the Jews, but no action."

"How did that situation finish up?"

"We'll call it a practice run for how I dealt with Dixon and his buddies. I can handle whatever this Ricker guy wants to dish out."

Palmer took a moment; he seemed to be thinking over his next words carefully. It seemed very unlike him, and even the two seconds of pause threw me for a loop. Finally he forced himself to speak. "What do you think of life here in our fair city?"

"Seems like there's a lot of pride, love, and yearning for Bernie Sanders. Not exactly my scene, but nothing to mess with unless there's a specific reason."

"You sound like every visitor we ever have."

"Is that a bad thing?"

"Not at all. In fact, I'd say 95 percent of the people here would be giddy to hear that's what you think of the town. Let me ask you this, then—what do you think of the history of our town?"

"Replace Bernie with Clinton or Kennedy and I figure it would be pretty much the same."

"And 95 perfect of the people here would be

giddy to hear that's what you think of their past. But the secret is that it ain't anything like that."

"It never is," I agreed.

"Stumptown, the Rose City, Bridgetown—Portland has had a lot of nicknames, but twenty years ago it was known as something else."

"What?"

"Skinhead City. This place could give a southern Klan rally or those Illinois Nazi punks that have been hanging around since the 60s a run for their money."

"Since when did all the skinheads delve into Portland?"

"Since Lewis and Clark sailed down the Columbia River. This place has quietly been as racist as anywhere in America. Oregon's first charter stipulated in not-so-subtle terms that the new state was for whites, and whites only. Your friends in the Klan were the biggest force around here—like anything you'd find in Jim Crow country. When blacks moved in during WWII to help with factory jobs during the war effort, the city made them stay in their own town up north—near the delta called Vanport. Don't go looking for it anymore, 'cause it's not there. When a flood wiped the place out it forced the black neighborhoods to finally move into Portland proper, at the disgust of the whites. Not exactly how MLK would have drawn it up, but shit happens.

"It turns out that still doesn't clean away the racist feelings for the next five decades. Oh sure, the civil rights movement eased things a little—but with the world watching hoses being used on protesters, and churches being bombed in Birmingham, why would anyone even notice what was happening in little ol' Oregon? We were over 600 miles from the closest major-league ball club at the time, and that was only when the Giants ditched the Polo Grounds. No one cared about Portland, and no one wanted to believe that racism on the West Coast was as bad as what was on the news each night.

"That feeling stuck around a few more decades, and while the Klan's influence waned, the racist punk skinheads took over. By the mid-90s they were running most of the bars in a huge swath of Southeast neighborhoods. You could walk into any one of them and find a few guys with swastikas, a large number of biker one-percenter patches, and all of them freshly buzzed up top, without a single minority in sight. It was like their own little playground."

"What's the point of telling me all of this?" I asked.

The marshal continued on without skipping a beat. "Then the 90s changed things around here. Grunge took over Seattle and the movement quickly expanded its counterculture ideas south to Portland. Soon we became a hip city, and everyone's been moving here since. Look at all these soccer fans singing songs about the Rose City. Most if not all of them weren't born here. They came from California and Colorado; they were escaping the bustle of New York. The harsh racism here had never even entered their minds. Almost by accident the increased numbers of out-of-towners started to lighten things up. Well, that and some police raids on the skinheads and their drug operations.

"Take Ricker's bar, for example. Back in 1997, the cops shut that place down through the RICO Act, just like they were doing for all the gangbangers in South Central LA. Using a law cops loved to enforce while shutting down black gangs to put an old-school Oregon racist like Ricker behind bars was just the extra kick in the pants. He spent the next fifteen years doing time, aligning himself with the Aryan Brotherhood to stay safe out in the yard, and allowing his hatred to simmer. He went from hating on anyone not white to wanting to wipe them out. He and his prison buddies were meticulous and planned to reclaim their city once they got out—only when that day arrived they found that the Southeast neighborhoods weren't anything like they remembered. Sure, the city is still more Caucasian than most, but it's gotten much better over the years. All the old bars and hangouts have been torn down to build gaudier apartment buildings for the never-ending influx of people we've had moving to the newest hip city and who never even thought Portland had a history of racism or segregation. The only skinheads left were the ones too stupid to even throw fifteen years at—and that lack of like-minded white power warriors forced them to run to the hills to get drunk and smoke and talk a big game without ever leaving their couch."

"Like our boy Dixon," I said.

"Only Ricker and his prison buddies don't take no for an answer. They moved out and set up shop in Idaho, where as long as they weren't housing the Unabomber no one would bother them. After a few years of getting organized they've started moving again to reclaim what they feel is theirs, but with so many out-of-towners running around the city now they need all the numbers they can get just to leave their mark—even if it means dealing with a bunch of worthless amateurs like the Nordic Hammers."

"That's a wonderful story and all, but I still don't see what any of it has to do with me," I said.

Palmer continued as if he hadn't even heard me. "Besides pride, love, and yearning for Bernie Sanders, today's Portland loves to take action for what it perceives as social justice—which is a very big problem for people like Ricker and his Hammers. A number of justice seekers organized into groups and started to spring up in places across the city— places with names like Portland for Everyone ... or the Portland Unity Coalition."

He said that last name with emphasis, and drove it home by giving me a hard stare.

"I know about your visits with Ms. Burkhart," he said. "She told me all about them. Which finally brings me to our mystery man Mr. Thorne here. How does a man walk into a place like the coalition and try to blackmail the woman running the place— a move I'd expect from the Nordic Hammers—to try and shut her down, but then drive over to Detroit and beat the shit out of three of the group's members without knowing he was putting himself in danger from a hard-boiled guy like Ricker?"

"Are you suggesting that I'm one of Ricker's prison buddies trying to shut down an anti-racism coalition while getting rid of the expendable help?"

"I want to say that really badly. It would make my job so much easier. But somehow that doesn't fit at all. You've got no tats, no swagger, and after my years of keeping tabs on guys like Ricker I've never even had a whiff of you anywhere. Even if I didn't believe your story about dealing with the Klan, you aren't a white supremacist. But you also aren't a bleeding heart liberal taking it to the street for social justice. You've most likely pissed off the killers within the Pacific Northwest's chapter of the Aryan Brotherhood while trying to steal money from one of the biggest problems the Brotherhood has seen around here in some time. All while sticking around the city for some reason I can't comprehend. So what exactly are you?"

"Does that question have to have an answer?"

"It can in court—on charges of trying to extort the Portland Unity Coalition."

I looked over at some of the soccer fans as a way to break the moment with the marshal. Trying to seem like I was more in the know, I took a moment. Then I asked, "What makes you think Ms. Burkhart is without sin herself? Why not take her to court and find out why she's got dealings with a known gunrunner and drug dealer?"

"I find that hard to believe."

"Oh, bullshit. If you know her well enough to know that I've paid her a pair of visits, you know how she's funding her little coalition. You really think something like that is working to end racist groups like Ricker and the Hammers because it says

Unity in the name? She's stringing you along so hard it would make a marionette jealous."

"Are you questioning her motivation to fight for this cause?"

"So far all I know is that she's pulled in donations from a drug dealer who was gunned down in his home a few days ago, in a scheme that's got money laundering written all over it. Tell me again how she's fighting the good fight for pride and love and Bernie Sanders."

"You mean the white woman who fell in love with a black man in the days when a lot of bars in Southeast were controlling the city against that exact thing? You mean the woman who had to suffer the worst pain anyone could imagine when those same skinheads shot and murdered her husband right in front of her eyes—putting enough bullets in him to make Al Capone feel like it was overkill, and through it all having to listen to the skinheads telling her that it was all for her own well-being? The same skinheads who said they had desecrated the body of her husband to snap her out of the spell that a black man had put on her and bring her back to the righteous world of whites only, in one of the most heinous crimes this city has ever seen? A crime that everyone in Skinhead City knew the motivations for—but no one was ever arrested or tried for? The wife who was devastated with the brutal loss of her beloved husband, and decided to do something about it herself, starting a coalition to end hatred from people like her husband's killers? Is that the woman you're accusing of being a front so she can launder money from a heroin dealer?"

Since the money laundering scheme was all I had, I tried not to be swayed. "Maybe you should go ask Ms. Burkhart's co-workers. But you can't, because they don't seem to exist. The only person ever there is Ms. Burkhart—only Ms. Burkhart. Seems like little can get done in changing the world when the whole organization is just one person."

"Maybe you should try visiting at different hours," Palmer shot back quickly. "Sure it's a small non-profit but you don't always need a big number of bodies to make a difference. Ms. Burkhart does a lot, and when she needs help she's always got her brother around."

"What brother? I never saw a desk for a brother when I was there."

"He's not exactly a traditional office kind of guy."

"So he's the traditionally untraditional kind of person Portland is known for?"

"He doesn't exactly have the kind of look you'd want to present when meeting with donors."

"What kind of look is that? Is he rocking a big Mike Tyson face tattoo or something?"

"No, not that." He chuckled. "You ever seen the movie True Romance? He looks like he's trying to be Gary Oldman, but on a skateboard."

"That motherfucker!" I shouted it loud enough that a number of soccer fans wedged nearby took notice. I stood up and raised my arms to show Palmer that I didn't intend anything violent toward him—but I also gave him a look to let him know not to try and stop me from getting to the exit. It worked—by the time I felt the sunshine of the Portland late-summer, he was still in his booth.

I caught the MAX train and headed back east to find the car. I had to head over to Chavez Boulevard. I finally had the connection to the Portland Unity Coalition.

CHAPTER 12

WHEN I GOT TO THE COALI-tion's office it was as if nothing had changed. No Gary Oldman wannabes were hanging around— Ms. Burkhart was by herself behind her small metal desk. I didn't even bother knocking when I came in. I immediately sat down in the same chair with the same charming grin. This time I knew the smile on my face was going to work because I finally had some cards to play. Ms. Burkhart kept the icy bitch look without saying anything. I decided to play her game. We sat in stubborn silence for what felt like forever to see who would flinch first. I knew my hand was better than hers this time around so I had no reason to bluff for the pot. It was her turn to break.

"You must be the stupidest person I've ever met." She had a way of going straight for the heart with the iciness in her eyes.

"My dear Ms. Burkhart. Why on earth would you say such a thing?"

"You've already tried twice to extort money from my hard-working charity, and gone home empty-handed to cry in your cheap beer, telling stories to your cheap crook friends about some woman who wouldn't play nice with you."

"I love a good Miller High Life when the moment strikes me."

"So what makes you think, this third time, that you are going to be any more successful? And what makes you think that I don't have the police already on their way here, to finally get you out of my hair?"

I kept my charming grin on her. I wanted her to sweat for a little longer, wondering what I had. "We both know that getting the authorities involved is only a last resort, so let's skip over that question. If you feel like you need protection I suggest you pull out your .25 again and keep it pointed at me. You can clearly see my hands are resting on this chair, so you'll have the drop on me if you feel a need to pull the trigger. Ah ... there it is. You certainly seem to hold that like a pro."

"Am I supposed to take that as a compliment from a low-life like you?"

"Ouch. Why would you say such nasty things to an old friend?" I was being as polite as I could.

"Yes, because we are such old friends." She was being as nasty as ever.

"So why haven't you introduced me to the rest of your family, Ms. Burkhart? Where is the rest of the Nichols clan?"

She didn't skip a beat when I dropped her maiden name. Probably figured it was easy enough to find with Google. "Is this what you are calling your newest idea to attempt to extort money from me? Unless Mr. Finn has been able to discover the cure for taking two bullets to the chest, I don't see what you're hoping to gain here this time around."

"Let's not talk about our mutual friend Mr. Finn. No, today I'd like to talk about another friend of ours: Mr. Nichols. He lives in the north quadrant of the city and loves nothing more than a soft couch and a freshly stuffed bowl. You know the man, Ms. Burkhart: your brother."

She didn't flinch for a second. "Last time you were here you tried to scare me with stories of someone named Ricker. Now you're trying to scare me with stories of my brother. Let me guess—this Ricker guy is the one who kicked down Jimmy's door and the reason he took flight without telling me where he was going? I don't see how any of this works with your pathetic blackmailing scheme."

"Actually it was my partner and I who kicked down Jimmy's door. I guess we chased him off, but that was when we were looking for Mr. Finn's money, which he owes to some very angry people back east. I was wondering how a group like the Portland Unity Coalition got hooked up with a gunrunner like Mr. Finn until I finally got my missing link. Your brother. My guess is you don't care or even know about Pete's gun running days, but a druggie like your brother would, and he'd know that Pete was trying to make himself into a big-time dealer with his ties to the Mexican cartel. Drug dealing isn't exactly a credit-card kind of business, so Pete must have been flush with cash and needed some place to put it. The money wasn't in his place and it wasn't at your brother's. Yet men with more anger than me have checked both places already, pretty sure that they were going to find the cash in one of those locations. Since we've now established that they were unsuccessful in their bids, it's not hard to go out on a limb and say there's only one other place it could be."

"And in the twisted reality you've made up in your mind, what are you going to do about it?" she scoffed. "Break my arms?"

"Considering the shit you've got me in without me being able to show anything for it, I'd say I might be in the right for something like that." I grinned at her again. Never tell the target everything you're going to do—that way, in their minds they will always jump straight to the worst-case scenario, and once they've done all the work of filling themselves with absolute fear they become much easier to open up.

"And what problems am I to blame for?"

"I came to the West Coast for a simple collection gig. Get in and out—maybe a trip to Voodoo Donuts, and then call it a day. Instead, I've got a fed on my tail, my partner is in the emergency room with tubes running out of his mouth, I'm on the shitlist of a white supremacist group that is more than likely looking to kill me, I've got an ice-cold bitch trying to stonewall me while aiming a .25 at my chest—and worst of all, I still don't have any dollars or donuts."

The icy bitch kept her icy glare on me but kept her mouth shut. Instead she adjusted the gun in her hand to a more comfortable position. I slid over in my chair to make sure that the barrel was pointed directly at my heart just in case her aim wasn't very good.

"You see, Ms. Burkhart, me and my partner were the first to get to your brother's door, but we weren't the only ones. Did you know after he fled the city, a member of a white supremacist group called the Nordic Hammers was seen trying to break into your brother's place carrying a .35 millimeter gun in his hand to take the money that he suspected was in there—after killing your brother? If anything, a thank you is in order—if me and my partner hadn't chased your brother out, he would have been just another murder statistic at the hands of an Oregon racist group."

"That's not how the police filed the report." She was clearly questioning my credibility. "What makes you think they were going to kill my brother?"

"I can assure you that it was the same .35 millimeter that was used to do in our mutual friend Mr. Pete Finn. If the gun was used to kill once, it'll be used to kill again."

She paused for a moment. I finally posted a point on my side of the scoreboard. Then she said, "You could be making all this up to scare me."

"You know I'm not. Think of it this way—there's a white supremacist group trying to find Pete's money for themselves. They started with him and ended the conversation pretty quickly. The next link in the chain was to your brother, who would have gotten the same fate if he hadn't already jumped ship somewhere because of me and my partner. And the next step after that? It would be the coalition he just so happened to work for that goes out of its way to fight the message that a group like the Nordic Hammers is trying to spread. So what makes you think they aren't coming after you next?"

"So your plan is to blackmail money from me, so when these Hammers show up at my door I can claim I've already been robbed and they need to go after you?"

"That's not my problem. I only care about my share. I've put my two cents in with the Hammers but I'm not looking for an all-out war with them. I just need my money and a flight back east, which gets me out of your hair. Then you can get back to fighting the Hammers any way you choose."

"And how do you suggest I go about doing that?" she asked.

"Just look at the wall behind you, with all your plaques and photos about the kind of world we can all live in together. I especially like the placement you have of the black man and white man together right behind your right shoulder. They look like real …"

I paused, looking at the photo.

"Look like real what?"

I stood up and slowly moved behind her desk. I suspected she kept the .25 on me, but I didn't bother to check. The picture was taking up all my attention. It looked like it had been taken nearly twenty years ago, and featured a white man and a black man posing like best buds, with an arm around each other, and smiling as if they were one big happy family.

The years hadn't been so kind to the white man. But his identity was easy to grasp. It was Marshal Palmer.

I pointed to the black man. "Who is this?"

"No clue."

"Bullshit."

"It's just a photograph someone took at a gala of ours. I thought it was a good way to impress potential donors as to our mission."

"Bullshit." Say it twice and the target knows you mean business.

"What do you want me to say then?"

I moved my finger to the white man in the picture. "Why do you have a picture of Marshal Palmer above your desk?"

"Is that who that is?" she said, trying to play it off.

I stepped up to her chair and leaned in until my face was inches from hers. I stared viciously into her eyes, but I gave her a moment to bring the gun up to my temple. "Who the hell are you?" I finally asked. "You're running a shady unity coalition that is getting funding from a heroin dealer and gunrunner with the help of your pothead brother, and in cahoots with a fucking federal marshal. Don't even try to deny that last part. It makes sense now how he got ahold of my number and how he always seems to be a step ahead of me. The good news for me is that your story keeps getting juicier for a newspaper reporter, who will have no problem bringing all of you down. Maybe I'll even drop a tip to Mr. Carter Williams, given the work he's done for me on this trip."

The icy bitch tried not to flinch. She tried to keep holding the gun steady to show she wasn't scared. To my surprise, she did it pretty well. After nearly thirty seconds of thinking it over, she finally made her move—and gently pointed the gun away from me and toward the desk. "You really have no idea what you're talking about, but you leave me no other option."

"And what does that mean?" I asked, feeling like I was finally getting somewhere.

"I want to hire you."

"Wait—what?"

"You have a going rate?"

"I'm not up for sale, lady. I've already got an employer back east. He's pretty fucking pissed at how much overtime I've been putting in out here."

"You want the money? Well, I've got it. It's not here in the office, so no point in going around tearing up the place to search for it. The only way you're going to get the cash is if you earn it."

"What kind of an offer is that? Two seconds ago you had a gun to my head, and now I'm supposed to trust that you'll pay me after my third attempt to get the money from you?"

"I could have pulled the trigger on you during the first two visits, but I didn't. How's that for trusting me?"

"Having a gun doesn't mean you have it in you to use it."

"What kind of damsel in distress do you think I am?"

"I'll give it to you that you're an ice-cold bitch, but how many people have you killed?"

"Two."

The coolness in her answer surprised me the most. Anyone could toss out a number to try and sound hard-boiled and bluff their way out. But I've dealt with killers before. Once they come to accept what they did, there's a calmness about it—almost like it wasn't a big deal. Never trust someone who excessively brags that they've killed someone. Ms. Burkhart however was like a female Bob Saginowski. Tom Hardy would be so proud.

"Shit. You're serious."

"Mr. Thorne, I believe I have given you an offer of employment without any explanation of the job itself. I should have mentioned that it might not contain the most legal of operations, but you shouldn't fear that I will turn you in to the authorities—federal marshals or otherwise. The only way to get you to believe me is to let you have something on me. So yes, I've killed two people, but don't go looking for it because you won't find any record of the incident."

I walked back around the desk and retook my seat across from her. "A hundred grand," I said, taking a wild shot. "You wanted to know my going rate—there it is."

"Done."

"You really have that kind of cash?"

"I stored it for Mr. Finn in a safety deposit box. I won't tell you which bank or which box, but if you already know the kind of cash he is supposed to have had, you'll know that I'm good for it."

"Before I agree to this proposition I want to know the whole story. Hundred grand or not, I'm not going to get myself involved in something without knowing what's waiting for me. I want you to spin the whole story—from Pete to Jimmy to Dixon to Ricker to Palmer to the coalition. And if there's any part I think you're holding out on me, I walk. If you're willing to hire me it means you're desperate. If I don't feel that desperation you don't have a deal."

She paused again to collect her thoughts. It was her tell that the icy bitch she put up as a front was finally hesitating and starting to give way to the real woman behind the desk. "What do you think of the city of Portland?"

"Seems like a city all about pride and love and yearning for Bernie Sanders."

"That's the kind of blissful thinking that gets trapped here. The more the people of this city think that's the case, the more the rest of the world does. And that's just fine with me."

"Instead of turning on the light and showing the ugly racism this place should be known for?"

"Used to be known for. Look around you—almost no one in Portland is actually from Portland. They all gladly fall into this bowl of ignorance that racism never existed here. If enough outsiders join our city with that mindset, they'll just make it a reality. Isn't that something to strive for?"

"It is, until guys like Ricker show up and start trouble, reminding everyone what the city once was and what it can be again," I said. She gave me another icy look, but I went on. "So riddle me this: what does a heroin-dealing gunrunner have to do with your idea of saving Portland from a race war?"

"Mr. Finn was quite an extraordinary man."

"Only man I know to run out on crime bosses and the mafia, all while dealing with the Mexican cartels. I'd say that's quite extraordinary."

"I never knew about his dealings in his life before he came to Portland, and to be honest, I really didn't care. It wasn't hard to guess he wasn't a choir boy just coming off a Rhodes scholarship—and it wasn't hard to see how good he was at getting his hands on black market guns."

I looked around at the empty office space. "To stock up your army here to fight off the coming skinheads? Doesn't seem very Bernie Sanders-ish."

"Quite the opposite. Because Mr. Finn was so adept at running guns, he knew how to keep them away from people with the intent to use them—people like the Nordic Hammers."

"Wait—so he was buying all the guns and not using them?"

"An effective way to prevent a race war—take away all the weapons."

"Sounds like your personal gun-control agenda. I always pegged you for a Democrat. How was he able to pull this off?"

"I never asked about his connections. The guy was a magician—he knew under which rocks to look for the kind of people who would be selling the weapons the Nordic Hammers wanted. And right when the group thought they had a deal, Mr. Finn swooped in with a higher offer and bought the arms right out from under them. A dumb-as-shit group like the Nordic Hammers never understood what was happening to them either. They thought it was just bad luck all the time."

I remembered the Instagram pictures of the whole crew passing around the one gun they had, and nearly none of them looking like they knew how to use it. They never had the arsenal to practice looking menacing. "Outside of Portland, this state is pretty rural, with gun shops all over the place. Hell, I passed one in the city itself today, over here on Foster. What's stopping them from loading up at a shop like that?"

"Ricker and the boys in Idaho won't let them go that route."

"What does Idaho care about the Hammers?"

"Idaho is the home of all of America's finest white supremacist groups. It's like their own West Point up there in some places, producing the best and brightest to spread the gospel."

"And Ricker got his education there?"

"Back in the 90s, he was one of their chief go-betweens for the skinhead groups here in Portland. He also knows that his fifteen-year prison sentence was partly due to gun-related charges. Sure, the NRA won't let the background checks go into effect. But the government isn't supposed to be using surveillance tactics on its own citizens, with or without a Patriot Act—yet that doesn't mean they aren't. So when Ricker got his name on papers for buying a bunch of guns that get used in numerous shootings, he got swept up in the RICO Act case, and to the slammer he goes. Never again for him. Black market and paper-free is the way to go for the Idaho boys."

"You're damn lucky Indiana is so far away."

"They've tried, but somehow Finn beat them to the punch there too."

"Yeah, he knows his way around the easy guns in Indiana," I sneered. "So then how was Finn able to afford constantly buying the guns away from the Hammers? They could just keep using the same money each time while Finn would always have to get a new stack of cash. Plus he had to be making enough to have at least a hundred grand in a safe-deposit box somewhere to pay me off—and considering how fast you took my offer I'll guess he's got even more stashed away in safety-deposit boxes across the city."

Ms. Burkhart kept her silence for a few moments, trying to think of the best way to tiptoe around the question, but for once my charming grin finally broke her. "My brother has never been the most moral of people. Nor the soberest."

"You can say 'pothead.'"

"If he's lucky enough to stay that way. He had little ambition in life after high school, and that turned into weed back when it was still illegal. That then turned into pills, and finally heroin. That was up until he met Mr. Finn a few years back. Mr. Finn had just gotten himself into town and was looking to set up shop. Befriending my brother got him hooked up with all the dealer connections he needed. Jimmy knew all the other users and players in the Portland heroin business; he was like a personal yellow pages for Mr. Finn. Pretty soon Mr. Finn became one of the biggest suppliers to the dealers in Southeast. He kept Jimmy on as his man on the street. Jimmy loved it. He got his supply of whatever drugs he wanted and got paid, too."

"Then why did your brother deny ever knowing Pete when I asked?"

"If a badass thug kicked in your door and demanded why you knew a heroin dealer and gun-runner, what would you say?"

That made sense—especially since it had been the second door-kicking incident Jimmy had had to deal with in two days.

Ms. Burkhart continued. "It was only later that Jimmy heard about his gun-running days and thought of the problems we were having at the coalition with the skinhead groups getting out of prison and trying to rearm themselves through the black market. That's when he introduced Mr. Finn to me."

"You are one fucked-up family," I said. I couldn't help myself.

"What kind of glass house do you live in?"

"One cracked from all the stones I've been tossing at it—but I'll still call you and your brother fucked up. One used Pete for drugs, the other for guns. You two were like Finn's wettest dream. How much of a druggie are you?"

"I refuse to touch the stuff."

"What the hell was Finn getting out of working

with you—if he was only spending money rather than making it?"

"Mr. Finn needed someone of good quality in the community to get enough places to safely hide his money. I volunteered to sign up at the banks as long as he agreed to use some of his ill-gotten income to spend on covering the black market himself, to keep the weapons out of the hands of the skinheads. With my work following the groups through the coalition I could alert him to who was looking to buy, and then he'd take it from there. But since I was now tied to him—hiding his money—he knew I couldn't rat him out for his heroin dealings for fear he'd turn on me and we'd all go down. A real marriage of convenience, you could say. Kind of like what we have here between us, Mr. Thorne. If we have dirt on each other, we can work together or go down together. But you don't seem like the sort of person interested in seeing what kind of iron bars we use here in Oregon."

"What the hell was Finn doing with all the guns he bought? He should have had the largest arsenal this side of the Rockies—but I didn't see anything in his house. And I doubt he's got deposit boxes for assault rifles."

"I don't know for sure, but last I heard he'd sell them to people outside the country."

"Shit—you mean the cartels?"

"Are you saying he worked for them?"

"With them, at least. Where do you think he got enough heroin to set your brother up with his own house? Those guys love untraceable weapons they can smuggle back to Mexico to shoot a snooping journalist or small-town mayor who tries to make a stand. He was probably buying his heroin shipments with black-market guns. Did you ever think of that?"

"Not my problem. I can't fix Mexico from here. But I can help save Portland by keeping the guns out of the worst racist groups in America."

"And what about all the heroin that you're helping to bring into the city? You're obsessed with stopping a race war, but turning a blind eye to a drug epidemic that has probably killed more people in Portland than any racist conflict ever could."

"Have you read the papers? Turned on CNN? Checked Twitter? Heroin is killing people in record numbers all over the country. In places like New Hampshire, and Ohio, and Kentucky. You know what never gets called out on that list? Oregon. Yeah, we've got drug problems—but who doesn't, right now? Ours is nowhere near as bad as other places across the country. But what if the number of dead we've got now is better than what it would be if we let a generation of just-liberated white supremacists get their hands on enough high-powered weapons to make an NRA convention jealous?"

"That's the most fucked-up thing I've ever heard."

"If Mr. Finn hadn't set up shop here with his heroin dealing, someone else would have. Sure we've got drug ODs, but without him, we would have had a different heroin kingpin, plus the possibility of a race war. If the options are drugs and the Hammers or just drugs, I'll take door number two every time."

"And just forget our journalist friends in Mexico?" I retorted. "You sound just ignorant enough to be from Portland. Shit, you people like to forget the rest of the world exists. As long as you hide your racism and brush over the past to tell people what a utopia this place can be, you don't need to look outside of your bubble."

"I'm only one woman, Mr. Thorne. I can't save the whole world, but I can damn well save a part of it."

"And this is all revenge for the murder of your husband?"

"I already got my revenge. I found those sons of bitches years ago and I shot them dead. I shot both of them right between the eyes. Then I tossed their corpses in the Willamette, where they were never found again. But you know the thing about revenge Mr. Thorne? It doesn't exist. I spent years wanting to hunt down and kill the two monsters who destroyed my life, and unlike the movies, where the screen fades to black and the credits roll, I still had to wake up the next morning to an empty bed. I killed two men who deserved what they got, and it didn't bring my husband back. There is no such thing as revenge in life. There's only a mission to keep this city together and make sure others don't meet my husband's fate. Isn't that a noble quest?"

"By dumping heroin into your city and helping run guns to cartels in Mexico?"

"I'm saving my city."

"In the most fucked-up way possible." I cursed at her. "If Finn was running all these shady operations for someone in an ivory tower like yourself, what the hell was he doing getting his name in the paper for dropping a huge donation to you?"

"He didn't."

"Bullshit. It was in the paper, with a photo of him dropping off ten large ones to your coalition."

"He didn't make that donation. It came from one of our other donors, at a fundraiser. But the local writer on her first-ever beat got her photos mixed up, and said the check he was handing over was for ten grand. His check in that photo was for much less, and done just to keep up appearances. It wasn't supposed to make news."

"So the shitstorm that's happened since I got here is because some college intern messed up a photograph?"

"Looks like that's all it takes."

I was so disgusted with her that I couldn't think about it anymore. "One hundred grand to protect you from Ricker and the Hammers. And the sooner the better—before I get caught any more in your ignorance. We'll keep in touch."

I stood up and walked out of the office.

CHAPTER 13

"SO THAT'S EVERYTHING," **I** told Anderson.

After leaving the coalition's office I had gone straight back to the hospital to check in on Dynamite. Considering the condition I had left him in, he was looking remarkably better. Part of that was due to the toughness that made him a menace in the ring. Another part was all the painkillers that were being pumped through his body. He was still all bandaged up, and with the way his knee looked it was doubtful he'd be able to dance in the ring again—but it was progress.

"She's one stone-cold bitch. She'd be a terror in the Golden Gloves with an attitude like that," Anderson joked.

"Yeah, but if we want to get the money for the bosses this seems like the best way. And technically what we'll get paid is from Pete's stash, so in the end it's a job well-done."

"As long as it turns into a job well-done. You seem to be overlooking what the job is. What exactly does protecting this woman from Ricker entail?"

"I figure we've got to get him behind bars somehow. If it were easy, though, our friend the marshal would have done it a while ago. So we might have to go through some unofficial or not-too-legal routes to get this done. We're pretty sure that Ricker killed Pete, and even if Pete was a scumbag, if we can prove Ricker did it, or some other kind of crime, it would get Ricker a long stretch, and out of the hair of the coalition. Then we're back east throwing down some oysters at Max's."

Anderson shifted uncomfortably in his bed. "You keep saying we, we, we on this. I don't see what I can do, stuck here. I think you're on your own for this one."

"Yeah, well—I've been meaning to talk to you about that. I've got an idea, but I don't think you'll be very excited to hear it."

"I'm already not. When was the last time an idea of yours actually worked out?"

"Well the first thing we need is to get Ricker out into the open—something he has proven very successful at not doing. Think about it: no one even knows what he looks like for sure, outside of some old mug shots during his fifteen-year stretch. If he's as smart as everyone keeps telling me, I'll bet the first thing he does is change up his look. We only know he's popped his head above water twice—once when he killed Pete, and once when he led his boys in your beating."

"That fucker." Anderson grimaced. "I never did get a good look at him, either. It was dark, and by the time I knew what was happening, the whole world was a blur."

"Yeah, but he doesn't know that."

"What are you getting at?"

"So here's the part you aren't going to like. You ever seen Jurassic Park?"

"Yeah."

"You remember the scene with the goat?"

"Oh, hell no!" Dynamite cut me off. "Fuck no! I'm not playing the goddamned goat waiting for some big-ass T-Rex while I'm sitting here in the hospital."

"Of course not! My plan was to have you waiting for the T-Rex outside of the hospital."

"You want me to leave the one place I'm safely guarded, so I can be bait for some batshit-crazy white supremacists?"

"Look—we need to get Ricker out into the open, and the only thing we know he needs right now is you, which is why it has to be you as the bait."

"Why the hell does he need me?"

"Because I'm going to head back over to Detroit and pay his Hammer boys a visit, to tell them that you're ready to talk to the cops with a video of the attack. Really juicy stuff that will get the five-O on them at any moment unless they pay a cool two hundred grand."

"I don't have any video of that night."

"Yeah, but they don't know that. All I have to do is tell them that as a black man in this city you always keep a body camera on you, in case you have a run-in with the cops. That grainy Rodney King footage will pop into their minds and they'll buy it."

"You think they'll go for the blackmail?"

"Of course not. The Hammers probably have fifty bucks between them. So they'll likely start following me in the hopes I lead them to you. Then we'll get you discharged from the hospital. When you're on the move in the outside world they'll strike. If they can shut you up for good, they'll be in the clear."

"But you'll stop them from doing that, right? Right?"

I tried to give him a reassuring smile, but it was as transparent as glass. It was an awful plan but it was the only plan we had.

"Oh shit," Anderson added. "With Pete no longer stopping them from getting guns, they've probably upgraded to the finest pieces and are looking to test them out."

"Yeah, that's probably the case."

"This is the shittiest idea I've ever heard."

"I told you that you wouldn't like it."

"And what's the endgame?"

"Well the best case is Ricker shows up and we take him down. Once that happens, then we get paid."

"In case you haven't noticed, I'm still hooked up to all these machines. I don't think they'll just let me walk out of here. Or even hobble out of here."

"Did you give them your real name?"

"Of course not. Dynamite isn't on a birth certificate anywhere, and Anderson won't be of much use—there's enough of us in the world that they'd never get a match. And I don't want anyone digging around in case they hit something I did back in Rhody."

"Exactly. So you're not getting this kind of treatment from insurance, but on Portland's dime. They'll be thrilled to get someone like you out of here and off their books. They won't put up much of a fight if you tell them you're leaving."

"What about that Hippocratic oath?"

"Doctors still get their paychecks from above. And when above isn't upset with you hobbling out, no one else will say otherwise."

"Shit. What happened to Obama's universal healthcare?"

"Got hijacked by the alt-right. Whole lot of racists and white supremacists in that group. Think of the good you'll be doing to get rid of people like that, so the next vote can get you back some of that sweet, sweet health care."

"You sure it has to go down like this?"

"If you've got any other ideas, I'm listening. Although I've got fourteen more voice messages from an angry boss back east—those are clogging up my ears, so you'll have to speak up."

"Wherever my burner is, the count is probably a lot higher. I want to go on record with my protest over this plan. But fuck it—let's get it over with."

"For the record, I'm not a fan of it either. You just hang tight. I'll be back after I make a visit to the Hammers."

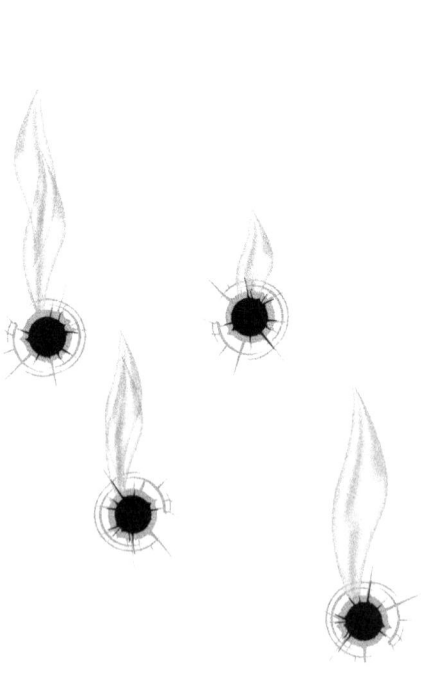

CHAPTER 14

"WHAT THE FUCK DO YOU mean he's got a video of us?" Dixon shouted.

We were standing outside his trailer in the middle of the day. I had staked out the place from the same location as last time. Twenty minutes earlier, I had watched the rest of his crew take off, leaving Dixon alone. I thought of Anderson's warning that the group was likely to have finally gotten their hands on some black-market weapons. I also thought about the beating I had given Dixon and his buddies on my last visit, and how if I played it right he wouldn't dare raise a gun to me, for fear that I might make it a second round. I told him so now, and that I had a proposition to make to him, laying out my terms: cough up two hundred grand in exchange for the body-camera footage.

"My partner doesn't take too kindly to the police brutality toward black men going around the country," I said. "He never goes anywhere without it now, just in case he gets pulled over for doing thirty-six in a thirty-five zone."

"Ain't the police supposed to be the ones wearing the cameras?"

"And they're also the ones who conveniently turn them off right when things get ugly. No chance, my partner says. He intends to film it himself to be sure everything gets on tape."

"So if he's got this video, and he doesn't trust the cops, what the hell is he going to do with it? You want me to believe he'll turn it in to the same people he was planning to film?"

"My partner would prefer not to have anything to do with the cops in case they find out what kind of record he's got. He says fuck 'em, but he also sees the opportunity to do some business, so here I am."

"For two hundred grand?"

"For two hundred grand."

"Fuck that! He ain't turning over shit."

"He doesn't have to. I hand it in instead. A white man who happened to find the footage handing over a hate crime in a city that's trying to get rid of its racist past? All I have to do is drop a line of where you live and then it's straight to the slammer for you and your boys. Do not pass Go, do not collect two hundred dollars. So what's it going to be? Are you going to pay up, or are you going to learn what happens to weak-ass Aryans in the slammer, surrounded by some of the most hardened gangbangers this state has to offer?"

Dixon thought for a moment—or at least tried

to give an impression of what he thought a thinking man would look like. "And you just want the money, and then you'll be gone?"

"Get out of this shithole state? With pleasure."

"Well, I ain't got that kind of money here. I'll have to go talk to the boys and get a collection plate going. Give me a couple of days."

"You've got two days to let me know." I threw a piece of paper at him—my burner phone number was on it. The only people with that number were the employer back home, a Golden Gloves champ, a US federal marshal, and now a dumb-as-shit white supremacist. Quite the collection of playmates I had found for myself.

It took a few more days to get Anderson out of the hospital— just enough for at least two dozen more angry calls from the employer. Apparently he had already gotten a stack of papers on his desk for jobs that I needed to collect on, but only after the Portland job was done. He also made sure to point out that he wasn't paying me any extra overtime for the mess that Pete Finn had started by being selfish and deciding not to deflect bullets shot at him.

I was a little surprised when after only two days I got a call from Dixon saying that he was having difficulty collecting the two hundred grand and was going to need a few more days. I made sure to keep an eye out for similar cars in my rearview mirror—but for all their stupidity the Hammers seemed to know how to tail a target. I could sense that they were out there somewhere, hiding from my sight. I had to applaud them for the effort.

The next day Anderson finally got himself out of bed without being shot up with painkillers, and decided today was the day to get it over with. He still looked awful, and he would never be as pretty again—or at least as pretty as a career of getting punched in the face can leave someone. The bigger concern was his knee—he had already come to terms with the fact that it would never work properly again. It was heartbreaking to see someone who had been so agile on his feet now have to lumber around with an awful limp, like one of those poor pro football players they like to show on the news, with stories about how the sport destroyed their lives. If we ever had to escape quickly on foot, the chase was going to be very short. But still Anderson wanted to get it over with.

"With the calls I've been getting from the boss back in Providence, if we do get shot down by these Aryan thugs, that'll be better than the alternative of getting chewed out again," he firmly said after I gave him one last chance to pull out of the mission.

"So you're 100% on this?"

"Fuck no. But I'm up and we're going anyways. Help me get in the car."

I opened the passenger-side door and gingerly helped Anderson swing his legs around to get in. Forget being chased on foot—if it came to it,

Dynamite would never even be able to leave the seat in time. So much for an escape plan.

I slowly pulled out of the hospital and tried to drive as casually as possible. It's one thing to act like you're driving naturally when following a client who owes the boss money and you don't want them to know what the rumpus is. It's another when you're the target and know there's a bunch of armed, angry, and stupid white supremacists ready to start firing at you from anywhere. Twice I almost ran through a red light because I was more focused on the cars around us, and which ones might be packing, than with the road straight in front of me. It wasn't until we passed Forty-Fifth Street on Powell that Anderson finally said something.

"That car has a replacement bumper."

"What?"

"There's a car three in front of us. That's not the original bumper. The paint doesn't match up right."

"Let me guess, white P.O.S. Olds?"

"Did you even have to ask?"

"What do you think it's doing in front of us?"

"Well the boys back in Providence used to pull a move like this. Find a main road they would think the target would go down and get a rabbit out in front. Then spring the trap from behind, because the first thing the target would do is hit the gas to try and make a run for it, smashing right into the lead car."

"Think these guys are smart enough to try it?"

"There's a P.O.S. Olds up ahead on a main road."

"Fair enough. You think Ricker is with them?"

"Well, only one way to find out."

I waited until we were about to cross over Foster Road, and hooked a tight right turn only after the Oldsmobile had already gone past the intersection. A garbage-green sedan and a beat-up blue pickup truck behind us made a similar last-second turn and followed us down Foster.

"At least we now know which ones are the bad guys," Anderson said. "Shit!" he added as the sound of gunfire rang out behind us. In the rearview mirror I could see two Hammers leaning out the windows from each car—one with a Magnum Desert Eagle and one with an assault rifle that looked to be one bump stock away from becoming a full-on machine gun.

"What the hell are they aiming at?" Anderson tried ducking low while keeping an eye behind us.

"Those dipshits have no idea how to shoot. They've probably seen enough car chases in the movies and think they can just aim and fire and we'll go up in some kind of big explosion."

"Man, they're going to kill a pedestrian with those things. Guns like that are inaccurate already, let alone at high speeds."

I leaned on the horn to warn anyone that I was about to blow through a couple of stop lights, when two black-and-whites with "Portland Police" on the side cut across from the side streets to make a perfectly executed blockade. I slammed on the brakes as hard as I could and nearly sent the pair of us flying through the windshield before coming to a full stop. I could have sworn that this was going to be the end, when a loud crash filled the air—only it didn't come from directly on top of us. Just to my left I could see the garbage-green sedan all crumpled up, as it had smashed into one of the police cruisers, which was now on its side and a smoldering mess. Wanting to avoid our sudden stop, the garbage-green had tried to swerve around us, but didn't see the sudden roadblock and smashed into one of the patrol cars. The Hammer who had been hanging out the window with the Desert Eagle was now yards down the road, having been thrown from the car on impact. He lay on the pavement with his head in a shape that was no longer round. The driver was still buckled into his seat, but had taken the full force of the crash. I could make out Dixon's look of surprise, as he still clutched the steering wheel, blood spewing out of his lifeless mouth.

Everything else in front of us was a swarm of moving parts and yelling. Cops were now racing around to the damaged patrol car—pulling out the driver, who looked hurt but alive. The pickup that had been following us had slowed down enough that when it swerved around us, it had enough time to avoid the other patrol car but not the lamppost. Police who had been out of sight came flying onto the scene with guns drawn, pointing at the pickup and pulling out the three Hammers, who were also hurt but moving.

It was only then that I heard the two other policemen—one on each side of our car, with guns drawn, demanding that we get out slowly.

"Keep your hands on the wheel!" one of them said. "I said keep them on the wheel! Slowly ... slowly! Do you fucking speaking English? I said slowly!"

I couldn't tell what the cop on the passenger side was saying to Anderson, who I guess was trying to alert them that he couldn't get out of the car with his knee in such bad shape. It felt like a dream being yanked out of the driver's side before being thrown face-first onto the hood. I think the cop was reading me my Miranda rights, but that could easily have been my memory of a TV scene—in reality maybe he was telling me to go fuck my mother for being involved in a chase that left a brother police officer in peril. All I could see in my mind at that moment was the bloody mess that was Dixon, and just how close Anderson and I had come to ending up that way.

Finally the cop pulled me up and spun me around to face him—and, much to my surprise, Marshal Palmer, who was giving the orders.

"This the guy?" the cop asked.

"Yeah, that's him. He's my CI."

"So what do you want me to do with him?"

"Can't let him blow his cover—you never know who is watching." Palmer was grinning at me. "In fact, it looks like he's trying to flee the scene right now."

"Flee what scene?" I tried to plead innocence but I knew it wouldn't get me anywhere. The cop unleashed a quick right hook to my gut, and while I was going down, he threw me into the side of the car, making sure my head hit every inch of metal on the way down.

When I finally hit the ground, the cop leaned in and whispered that he was only putting a beating on me to make sure no one thought I was working for the marshal. That included me too.

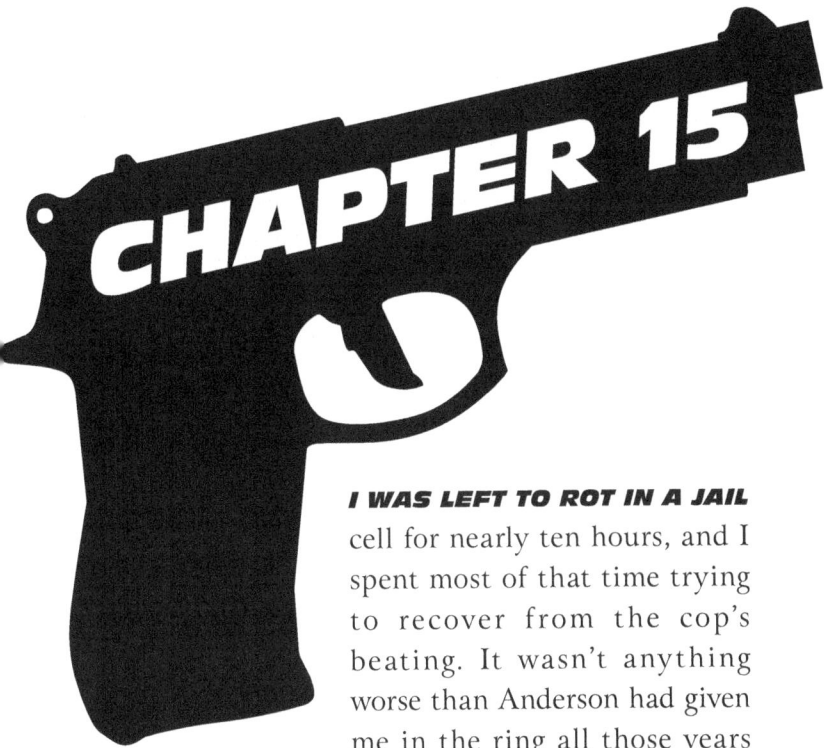

CHAPTER 15

I WAS LEFT TO ROT IN A JAIL cell for nearly ten hours, and I spent most of that time trying to recover from the cop's beating. It wasn't anything worse than Anderson had given me in the ring all those years ago, but I was no longer young enough to bounce back with just some Advil and a couple chasers of lousy scotch.

Eventually I was helped out of the cell and taken to an interrogation room, where I was handcuffed to the table—as if I could run anywhere anyways. When the door opened, Palmer strolled in alone, with the biggest grin I'd ever seen from him.

"Well, well—Mr. Thorne, is it?"

"Cut the shit. Where's Anderson?"

"Mr. Anderson?"

"My partner in the car."

"He's back in the ER, where he should have been the whole time. Don't worry—we didn't do a thing to him. But he's still in terrible shape from before. What the hell were you doing pulling him from the hospital like that?"

I didn't find enjoyment in someone doing a spot-on impersonation of my father, and decided to jump right to it. "You come to pay me my cut?"

"Your cut?"

"Since apparently I'm a CI working for you, don't I get something for helping you pull in some of Portland's most wanted?"

"You mean like a bounty hunter? Didn't we talk about how the state of Oregon doesn't do bounty hunters?"

"So what does being your CI get me?"

"Well, to be a CI for me you've got to have signed on beforehand. Funny thing—it seems I've misplaced the paperwork."

"I didn't know there was paperwork to sign." I didn't need his condescending jokes either.

"How about instead of getting your share of the bounty, you get the ability to remain alive, and we'll call it even? Now tell me—what the hell were you doing out there?"

"How did you know where we were?" I shot back.

"We've been following you. I saw you at Dixon's place from a distance the other day. I saw you waiting for his boys to leave before you went in. Looked like you were having a friendly conversation this time, since you didn't leave him with any kind of beating."

"Your cop buddies pulled out in front of us. How'd you know where we were going?"

"When I put the pieces together that you were pulling Anderson out, I figured you were going to make a run for it away from the Hammers. You'd only know two hiding places in the city. One was Jimmy's place in North Portland—the other was Finn's in Southeast. So I covered both—but I figured you'd avoid showing your face at Jimmy's again, and put my money on Finn's."

"What happened to the Hammers?"

"You won't hear from them anymore."

"Why do you say that?"

"Your boy Dixon is quite dead—as is his buddy, who tried doing his best Superman act, but ended up worse than Christopher Reeve falling off a horse."

"And the rest?"

"Besides the two dead, we've got three under arrest in the hospital. There was also a another car not involved in the crash that we had been keeping tabs on—and what do you know, it was loaded with illegal firearms that should put them all away for quite some time."

"And Ricker?"

Palmer clammed up at the name. "He was a no-show."

"Who was in the Olds then?"

"What Olds?"

"There was a P.O.S. Oldsmobile driving ahead of us that belonged to Dixon. Had an ill-fitting bumper on the back. If you've been scoping out his place like you've been saying, you know the one I'm talking about."

"We didn't pull over any Olds of any kind."

"I saw it. Ask Anderson—he saw it too."

"Did you see who was driving it?"

"No—but I was surprised to see Dixon dead in the green car when I thought it was him in the white one ahead of us before all hell broke loose."

Palmer took a moment to look over some notes in a folder he had in his hands. Finally he snapped and threw everything down. "Shit! He was right there, wasn't he?"

"Ricker?"

"We had him. He was right there. It had to be him. We got everyone else."

Finally I got to smile at Palmer's misfortune. "Looks like it's bad news for you, then."

"That's still bad news for you as well."

"What the hell are you talking about? You can't charge me with anything here, CI or not. There's no law against getting a friend out of the ER when it was his choice, and running all those red lights was due to our running for our lives. In case you hadn't noticed, there were two cars full of guys with illegal firearms, trying to gun us down."

"I'm not talking about police work. You've still got a job to finish for Ms. Burkhart."

"What part of that operation are you involved with, exactly?" I tried to sound as arrogant as possible. "Are you with the gun-running side of things, or the heroin dealing?"

"The part that cleans this city up from its racist past by keeping away the kind of thugs who spend their time daydreaming that one terrorist act is going to spark a race war."

"So you're helping a heroin dealer peddle his trade?"

Palmer took a deep breath to try and calm himself before looking me right in the eyes. The sense of honesty he was about to speak felt solid enough to touch. No more Dad impersonation here. "Michael Burkhart was my best friend since we were in middle school. We stayed close even when I went to the academy and he took the bar. Hell, I even set him up on a date with the woman who would eventually become his wife. This was back in the days when this city was nearly as segregated as anything you'd have seen in George Wallace's dreams. The blacks stayed in the Alberta neighborhood and the whites got the rest. I've seen what this city has become—from its awful racist past to the present that it always had the chance to be. It still ain't perfect—and maybe it never will be—but it's a hell of a lot better than what it was, and in many cases better than anywhere you'll find in the whole US. Michael would have loved it. He fought like a terrier for this kind of city—both growing up on Alberta and in the courtroom. If I get the chance to stop these racist assholes from coming to my town, and if I can put them back in cages before they get to make any more Burkhart widows, sign me up."

"Does the US Marshals Service know you're doing that with the help of a woman who's allowing heroin to run through the streets of this place?"

"The US Marshals Service is interested in my helping to apprehend wanted criminals who have skipped out on their court dates or are avoiding warrants issued across state borders."

"That works out conveniently for you when those looking to bring back the dirty past of Portland are being sent in from Idaho."

"According to federal law that isn't convenient at all. But then again that's what the marshals are here for."

"So why not just take him down yourself ... unless ..."

"Unless what?"

"Oh yeah, I get it now," I said, smiling back at him as the pieces started to come together. "Ricker isn't technically wanted by the marshals, is he? Oh sure, he did his time from the RICO cases back in the 90s, but he's good and knows how to keep himself out of the spotlight when charges finally come around. That's why he's been getting his Hammer boys to do all the dirty work for him. He's never been around to buy the weapons, but of course the Hammers keep messing that up. When they chased us today, it was Dixon and his crew shooting our way, while Ricker stayed in front with an easy escape route when you all showed up. Hell, even his RICO case and prison time were in Oregon, so he hasn't been crossing state lines that you know of. All you can do is convince your superiors that he's the kind of guy who might be up to something, and since he's got a violent record from two decades ago you should at least be keeping an eye on him. Surveillance, but no action until you've got something solid. Am I barking up the right tree here?"

He shifted on his feet uncomfortably before finally blurting out, "Unless you know of any crimes we can pin on him."

"How about the murder of Pete Finn?"

"You sure about that?"

"Yup."

"How do you know?"

Even if the marshal was trying to be on my side, I decided it best not to give away too much information to a federal authority about how I came to find a dead man after I had broken into his home. "Can't tell you."

"Maybe he got one of his Hammers to do it for him?"

"You saw how those guys shoot. You really think they could have put a couple of tight ones into Pete like that?"

"You seem to know a lot about the untimely death of Mr. Finn. How do I know you didn't kill him and now you've found a perfect scapegoat for the job?"

"What would I still be doing in this city then? Kill the guy and then hang around to get beat up, shot at, roughed up, interrogated, hassled by a federal marshal, and blackmailed into a job by a bitch of a woman?"

"Blackmailed? Weren't you the one trying to do the blackmailing?"

"Let's call it fair that I didn't shoot Pete."

"Then what evidence have you got to help me get this on Ricker? A murder weapon would be lovely."

I also decided it best not to explain to him how

the gun ended up in the bottom of the Willamette. "Can't help you there."

"Well, then, it looks like my hands are tied. Nothing I can do but continue to work surveillance for our friend Ricker—although now that his gang of patsies is pretty much done for, we'll have to start all over again for leads."

"Try looking for a P.O.S. white Oldsmobile with an ill-fitting bumper."

"Why don't you try looking for it yourself? If you want the cash from Ms. Burkhart, you've got a job to finish. We both know Ricker is dangerous, and if he's come back to Portland once, he'll come back again. Nothing I can do about it except maybe look the other way if there's a third party involved."

"Because I'm a CI of yours now?"

"I'm not obligated to talk about who is or isn't a CI of mine."

"Or to get your hands dirty where it might make it look like you've got a vendetta against someone like Ricker."

"You've got a job to finish." He picked up the papers and walked out the door.

CHAPTER 16

THEY LET ME STEW IN THE cooler for a few more hours before finally letting me go. That was fine by me, as it gave me a few more hours to heal up, as well as a few more hours to think quietly about what the hell my next move was going to be. When I was finally released and walked out the front door of the police station I still didn't know my next move—but it turned out my next move found me. The burner phone in my pocket started to ring, displaying a number I had last seen when Dixon called me a few days ago. I'd never had a dead man call me before, and figured I had better answer.

Once I was far enough away from the station's front door I answered. "Hello?"

Only silence.

"Hello?" I said again. This time I was greeted by a muted sound of heavy breathing, like the caller was trying to hide themselves while still letting me know they were there. Finally, I snapped. "Cut the shit, Ricker. I've had a really hard day and the last thing I need is you trying some Zodiac shit on me."

The breathing stopped for a moment, as if he was trying to say something. I decided to keep the conversation going.

"Look, it was your boys who came after me. They don't know how to shoot. Their deaths are on themselves, not on me."

The breathing picked up again before a very calm voice spoke on the other end. He was going out of his way to show that he was in control of the conversation, but he really didn't need to. He seemed to be naturally able to choose words that were short and poignant—something a man who normally feels in control of a conversation already does without having to show it with the added emphasis of the tone of his voice. "Who the hell are you?" he said.

"Malcolm X."

"Who are you?" he said again.

"Matthew Scudder."

"Who are you?"

"Are we going to keep going round and round in circles like this? If I wanted to tell you, I would have on the first try."

"Okay, Mr. Malcolm X Scudder, what kind of deal have you cut with the cops?"

I laughed. "You think I'm working for the cops?"

"How did you know who was calling?"

"I figured that it wasn't Dixon calling me from the beyond. You are the only one who could have his phone. You probably found it in his car when you drove it to keep an eye on your goons as they tried to take out me and my partner. Don't try to deny it—I know it was you in the Olds ahead of us. And since you seem like someone who keeps his hands clean of a dangerous situation by watching from afar, I knew you would follow us to the police station and see who came out a free man."

"If you're so smart, what makes you think I don't have you right now in my rifle scope?"

"Because it's broad daylight and you wouldn't risk it. I'm guessing that the fifteen years you did really put a hurt on you. Took your city away from you—and by the time you got out you had to go hiding in the sticks of Idaho. The last thing you want is to go back behind bars. You've been too damn careful to make sure nothing gets tied back to you. Gun me down right now, in front of a police station? Too many witnesses and security cameras around. You'd never have a chance."

Ricker laughed. I hadn't expected that. "You sure sound like someone working for the cops."

"Would a guy getting paid by the cops be looking to make a score selling the video of you and your Hammer goons beating up a black guy?"

"Why would I care about a video like that?"

"Because it would hold up in a court of law, connecting you and the Hammers, who are now all in prison. Sure they might say Ricker made me do it, but there really isn't any hard evidence of you collaborating with them is there? Well, except for the night you all put a whupping on my partner."

Still in control, he didn't even pause to think it

over. "So, what—you're going to blackmail me for two hundred grand?"

"Two hundred grand? That was before you sent your goons to try and gun me down. That's gonna cost you. With the rate of inflation these days, I should charge you half a million at least, just on principle. But I'm guessing you don't have anything close to that—and since I'm such a nice guy, I'll give you a one-time deal and make it half of that. Two hundred and fifty grand. You get the tape, I get the hell out of Portland, and we all get what we want. Does that sound like something I'd do if I was working for the cops?"

"How can I trust you?"

"Did you see the beating those assholes dished out when they were cuffing your crew? If the cops wanted my help they wouldn't have bashed my head in like that."

"That did give me a smile. That's the way cops should deal with anyone working with the mongrels destroying the white nation God intended for us."

"Black, white—I don't care. Only color I'm interested in is green. You've got three days to get back to me for the meeting place." I hung up on him, finally taking back some control in the conversation.

CHAPTER 17

I HEADED OVER TO THE HOS-pital to check in with Anderson, who now had both uniformed and plain-clothed police outside his room. I couldn't tell if they were on security duty in case anyone else from the Hammers showed up to finish the job, or were there to prevent me from talking the patient into walking out again. Either way, they gave me scowling looks when I showed up, but still let me into the room. Anderson was hooked back up to machines that checked his heart rate, and had a tube attached to his arm for painkillers any time he needed them. He was alert in the bed, watching whatever soap opera was on Univision at the time.

"I didn't know you spoke Español," I said, greeting him.

"I don't, but this shit is crazy when you're hopped up on these meds. Man, I can't keep track of which twin is back from the dead to steal his brother's wife. Or is it his father's new wife? They speak too damn fast to follow."

"How are you holding up?"

"Better than ever."

"That's not just the meds saying so?"

"Hell, no. Cops treated me like a king, getting me out of the car and back here to rest. Too many people with video capabilities on their phones looking for one mistake by a police officer being too rough with a suspect—something to paste all over the internet. Especially being a black man with an all-white police crew. I got handled with kid gloves. I could get used to pampering like that. What about you?"

"I got my head dribbled like a basketball. It left dents on the car all the way down."

Anderson laughed. "Deserved."

"I'll have you know it hurt more than the whupping you gave me in the semis."

"That was just your head, though. I remember popping you with plenty of body shots as well."

"Yeah, yeah, yeah." I don't always have a comeback for something that is so true. "I got a call from Ricker earlier today."

"Oh, yeah? How'd that go?"

"Well, he called me from Dixon's phone."

"How do you know it was Ricker then?"

"Dixon's dead."

"No shit?"

"Yeah. He was gone on impact, driving the car that came flying over on my side. I saw his face bleeding out before the cops and Palmer pulled me out."

"What about the rest of the Hammers?"

"They're pretty much done. The gunman in Dixon's car took a long flight with a short stop."

"I saw him bounce face first off the pavement," Anderson commented.

"The rest got rounded up by Palmer and Portland's finest."

"So you think it's just Ricker now?"

"That's my guess."

"What did he want?"

"He was sniffing around for information."

"What did you tell him?"

"Palmer made it pretty explicit when I talked to him at the station that I'm still on the hook with Ms. Burkhart for the cash we need to get out of here. So I've got to keep tabs on Ricker and meet him in person somehow. I told him that if he wants the video I offered the Hammers, the price had been raised."

"The video that doesn't exist?"

"The Hammers came after us for it, and Ricker still sounded interested when I gave him a second chance. So I'd say he believes that it exists."

"So the plan is to blackmail a dangerous white supremacist killer with a video that doesn't exist, getting him arrested in order to get a payoff from a woman you failed to blackmail earlier? You really know how to make a mess of things."

"Me? What would you have been doing?"

"I was just keeping an eye on things when this big-ass white boy kicked down the door of the guy I was watching."

"Sure, let me take the fall for this. How would

you have proposed to get your money off of Pete, when you knew that he was already dead?"

"That's all in the past, so it doesn't matter now."

"If you're such a world-class planner, tell me, five-star General Patton sir, how would you deal with this Ricker situation?"

Anderson shut off the television and gave me his full attention. "Does Palmer or anyone else know Ricker called you?"

"Nope, just you."

"You think he's still cruising around in that P.O.S. Olds? If Dixon was driving a different car I'm guessing that was him ahead of us when the shooting started."

"I figured out too that it was Ricker ahead of us when I saw Dixon in the green car. But I'd wager he's ditched the ride and found something else. He's been too paranoid to have even the slightest piece of evidence come back to him. Even a car near a shooting but not actually involved in it would be too much heat for him. Plus he called me as soon as I walked out of the station and claimed he had a rifle on me. That means he had to be nearby. But I didn't see a sign of any white car, let alone one with a messed-up bumper."

"So that piece of intel is out."

"I'd say as out as disco."

"Well the only way you're going to take him down is if you meet him face to face, and the only way you're going to do that is if you show up to offer the video that doesn't exist. But you're going to have to shake the cops first before you do so."

"What do you mean?" I asked.

"If this Ricker guy has gone to such great lengths to be cautious, I'm sure he's keeping an eye on you, figuring either you're working for the cops or they're tailing you. The PD has already shown they had a hook on you, which is how they knew when to pull out with the roadblock and take down the Hammers. Just because they let you out of jail doesn't mean they aren't still watching you. And if Ricker saw you walking out of the station, he's probably figuring the same thing."

"So I have to set up a meeting with a known killer, but first ditch my guardian angels?"

"It's the only way. Think you can shake them?"

"It was a lot easier to lose people in Hartford, when I knew all the roads. But I'll figure something out."

"You think you can handle Ricker?"

"I still don't even know what he looks like. You didn't catch a glimpse of him when they put you in here, did you?"

"Sorry—I was a little too preoccupied with getting my knee bashed in."

"That still leaves us in the same situation. It's either face him down or get chewed out by the employer so badly that I wish I was dead. Tough choice, to be honest."

"Maybe it's best then to stay here and let Ricker go. Screw the hundred grand and let the bosses deal with it themselves." Anderson sighed, looking down at his broken body. "I'm clearly going to be worthless to the boys back in Providence now. Ain't no one going to be scared of someone who can't even walk straight. I can't even catch up to anyone with a hobble like this, let alone put the fear of God in them with my fists."

"We're too deep into this already. Ricker was supposed to come out here to shape up the troops for when their race war was going to ignite this city again. Instead, all of his crew are either dead or locked up. I don't think Idaho would be happy to hear that a guy who has wasted fifteen years in prison has made things even worse—I don't think they'll give him another chance. He needs a pound of flesh to show that he can get results, and since he's already come after us a couple of times with guns and beatings, I doubt he will stop without finishing the job. And I'm not the kind of guy who likes to look over his shoulder."

"You think you can do this alone, then? You know if I was able to, I'd be out there with you."

"I'll throw in a couple of your favorite right hooks when I get my hands on him—just for you."

"Don't let it go to the judges. Finish him before the bell."

Anderson stuck out his hand slowly, and I shook it with a knowing nod—there was a very good chance we'd never see each other again. It would be a shame to come to the end just when I had found a partner in the business like him.

CHAPTER 18

I SPENT THE REST OF THE day going through Google maps and checking out different locations I could offer up to Ricker for a meeting place. I walked along the east bank of the Willamette River, liking the idea of having the face to face nearby.

I knew I was going to be alone but I couldn't trust Ricker to not bring backup. If we did it along the river, I could have my back to the Willamette. I'd only have to worry about what was in front of me—there was no chance someone could jump me from behind. I'm no math wizard, but 180 degrees of danger sounded a hell of a lot better than 360.

I stayed on the east side and swerved through some of the narrow neighborhood roads, timing how long it took to get from street to street as I put together a map in my head. I couldn't practice the route entirely, remembering what Anderson had said—that the cops were probably keeping a tail on me the whole time. I didn't want them to see the rehearsal before the curtain went up on opening night.

The plan still sucked. There were too many gaping holes where I was sticking my neck out for no reason. But it was the only plan I had, and the clock was ticking. If Ricker thought I had the video, he'd have to play along for now. But if I waited too long he'd figure I was bluffing, and then he could come at me whenever he wanted. All he had to do was track down Anderson, who wasn't moving from the hospital. All I had to trump that was the promise of a video I didn't own, for cash I knew he didn't have.

Later the next day, I called Dixon's number four times before Ricker finally answered. He pulled his Zodiac breathing act again. Not "Hello." Not even "Wazzup?" Just that damned evil sound.

"We make the switch tomorrow," I said.

"No. We make it tonight."

"Hell, no. I've got the video—we play by my rules."

"I don't trust your rules, which is why we do it tonight. Tomorrow you might bring the whole PD with you, and I'm not having any of that. No, it's tonight—before you can rally your troops."

I hesitated for a moment. "Fine."

"Speaking of which—you better make sure you lose the cops before you show up. If I catch even a whiff of the police who have been following you since you left the station, I'm dumping the money in the river, and you'll never see a cent of it. Then I'll hightail it out of here, leaving you with jack shit. You got it? This is on you."

"Since there'll be no cops and we're doing it at your time, we're doing it at my place."

"Depends on the spot."

"Underneath the Sellwood Bridge there's a park that runs along the river on the east side, just before you get to that small amusement park. At night no one should be there, and it's dark enough to get us in and out without being seen."

"I know the place. 3 a.m. No cops." He hung up.

I moved over to a different hotel room in Gresham, trying get away from it all and clear my head for what was going to happen later that night. I tried to play all the angles, but there were just too many. What if I couldn't shake the cops? What if Ricker brought in reinforcements? What would happen if Ricker actually brought the money? What would happen if he patted me down for the body camera? What if I was walking into an ambush? I opened the bottle of White Label I had bought and took a really deep swig.

I had always enjoyed the loan-sharking business. Dealing with the employer was a pain in the ass, but mostly I was free to get the jobs done on my turf. Usually it was pushover losers who needed the fear of God put in them to let them know they needed to start paying up. I rarely ever even needed to throw punches to get my point across. Just my looks got the job done. But that wouldn't be the case tonight.

Ricker wasn't a desperate man a few weeks late on a shady loan payment. He was a known killer, now with the ability to arm himself with whatever hand cannons he wanted, looking to end me on his turf, in his city. Or at least the city he remembered from more than fifteen years ago. As a Hartford boy, I was out of my league.

I took another big swig and called the employer back for the first time in two weeks. He welcomed me with a barrage of curses that would have made a sailor blush. After three minutes I finally spoke. "I'm getting your money tonight. If you don't hear back from me by tomorrow night, check the obituaries." I hung up. Fuck him—it was time to roll.

When the clock changed over to 1 a.m., I decided to put my plan into action even earlier than I originally anticipated, just as an excuse to stop sitting around and thinking of everything that could go wrong. I cruised around some of the neighborhoods around Seventy-Fifth Street off of Powell just to get a sense of who was trailing me. A couple of sharp turns left me with at least two black sedans as prime targets to be my police escorts for the evening. I hopped it back onto Powell, taking it to Fifty-Second Street, and rolled into the Taco Bell drive-through. This was a double-whammy of genius, as it forced those following me to expose themselves—by either getting in line or waiting nearby. It also rewarded me with a couple of shredded chicken burritos and some triple-layer nachos. This specific Taco Bell had the added bonus of being one of the slowest service windows in the Pacific Northwest, giving me even more time to spot one of the black sedans waiting across the street. The other one was now two cars behind me—meaning he was stuck in the slowest lane ever once I peeled it out of there.

I hooked a right and started toward Thirtieth Street, to enact my plan. The one black sedan that wasn't stuck in the drive-through was still in pursuit. The neighborhood streets in eastern Portland are only wide enough for three cars to get through; this drops down to one when there is street parking happening in both directions. Slowly making my way without hitting anything, I saw that no other cars had followed us since the Taco Bell stop. They must have thought I was ignorant to their game.

After a few more turns I finally came to my moment of truth, where the street stops being a two-way road and turns into a one-way street going in the opposite direction with a big a "Do Not Enter" sign. A Portland specialty. Looking around the streets at 2 a.m., I could tell that no other cars were coming. It was time to gun it. Pulling off my best Dale Earnhardt impersonation, I peeled past the "Do Not Enter" sign and raced up the narrow street going the wrong direction. Since I had been followed all day in unmarked cars, I guessed that the cop behind me had been given instructions not to give himself away under any conditions—which meant the trailing sedan now sat at the intersection, dumbfounded.

Once I was far enough away, I hooked a quick left and shut off my headlights, blending into the night. I drove a few more blocks and made a hard right, followed by another left. Eventually I was able to work my way over to Belmont without anything showing up in my rearview mirror. Ricker's demand that there be no cops had been taken care of.

Once on Belmont I headed west toward the river, and caught 99E, going toward the Sellwood Bridge. By the time I got there it was nearly 2:45 a.m. There's a parking lot for Waterfront Park, but not wanting to alert anyone to my presence, I stashed the car on Tenino Street and hoofed it the five blocks over as quickly but quietly as I could. Once I got close enough I made out someone's silhouette near the small restroom area in the parking lot. With swiftness I haven't felt since I was last in the ring, I let my feet carry me toward trouble. The silhouette seemed anxious, constantly looking around toward the road for me to show up. Instead I doubled back along the river and approached him from behind.

"You looking for something?" I said, grabbing him by the back of his collar.

"You got the video?" he asked, quietly. Still being held by the collar, he turned slowly to look me in the eyes. He was shorter than I expected, rather scraggly in the face, and desperately in need of shave.

"First the money, Ricker," I said.

It was my downfall. I heard a gun cock behind me. I was so intent on getting the drop on the silhouette I had failed to check if there was anyone waiting to get the drop on me. Then I heard the Zodiac breathing—but this time clear and in person. Like the cocked gun, it was coming from behind me.

"There ain't no money, because there ain't no video," Ricker said, holding the gun steady just behind my head.

"You don't know that."

"You don't know what I look like, do you? You can't tell the difference between me and some homeless guy I paid twenty bucks to sit here and wait for you. If you can't tell who I am, why are you trying to sell lies that you've got evidence against me?"

"For the cash," I spat.

"I'll ask again—who the fuck are you?"

I didn't answer.

I could feel the gun still on me so I didn't move. That gave him an opportunity to show that he had a crowbar in his other hand—he slammed it right into my ribs. Golden Glover or not, I was going down. As soon as I hit the dirt, the homeless man took off into the night, leaving me in a heap, with Ricker standing over me, ready to take another swing.

"You and your darkie boyfriend show up and stop my crew from killing off that Nichols scumbag. Then you show up and put a whupping on my boys at their own place. Then you try to blackmail them. Then you get them all busted or killed. I can't figure out for one damn second what the hell any of this matters to you."

"I don't care what you want," I wheezed out, ribs aching while I tried to get back to my feet.

Ricker wound up and slammed the crowbar into my back this time, flattening me out on the ground again. "Are you some kind of fucking goody two-shoes thinking this town doesn't belong to my kind?

Get the picture: Oregon has been, is now, and always will be for whites only! You may have the skin color but you're a damn disgrace to the Aryan race."

"I told you, I don't care about any of this. I'm just here to get my money."

"What money? There isn't any. I knew your bullshit about the body camera wasn't real."

"I'm here to collect on the money Pete owes."

"Pete?"

"Yeah, Pete."

"Like, Pete Finn? You know he's dead, right?"

"Of course I do. You're the guy who put two in his chest for blocking your boys' gun deals on the black market."

"How do you know so much about me?"

"You aren't as slick as you think."

"You don't even know what I look like." He swung his foot this time, and caught me with a vicious kick to the side of the face. "And I guess you never will."

I rolled over on my back, trying to regain my vision. All I could see was the barrel of a .44 Desert Eagle aimed between my eyes.

"The Nordic Hammers tell you to burn in hell," he said.

Two gunshots went off. I thought it was the end, except I didn't feel any holes in my chest. Instead the Desert Eagle started listing to the right and the sound of a body hitting the ground brought me back to reality. I tried to sit up, and saw Ricker dead, still holding the gun and the crowbar, with what looked like two .25-caliber slugs in his face.

Another silhouette walked out of the shadows, but this time I knew it wasn't the homeless man. Ms. Burkhart was still holding her gun, and stood over the corpse of the white supremacist. In a rage she unleashed four more rounds into Ricker's dead face, completely disfiguring him. She only stopped when I finally was able to stand up and grabbed her arm gently to bring her back from her anger.

"Help me out," she said, keeping in charge of the situation. "Grab one of his legs. Let's toss him in the river. I'm sure someone will have heard the gunshots and called the authorities."

Still in a daze from my beating, I did what she said—in no time we had tossed the disgusting bloody corpse into the river and watched it float downstream. She kept watching the body until it disappeared from view. Then she asked, "Why did you stop me from shooting him some more?"

"He was already dead. Seemed like a waste."

"My husband got more rounds than that put into him."

"And where does revenge like that get you?"

"I still wanted to put more in him. He killed Pete. He tried to kill Jimmy. He tried to kill you and your partner. He was going to come after me. He thought he was so smart, using his cronies and keeping himself clean while pulling the strings for his racial violence. He should have gotten more bullets."

"C'mon." I nodded toward the road to get us away from the river. "Let's get out of here before we're seen."

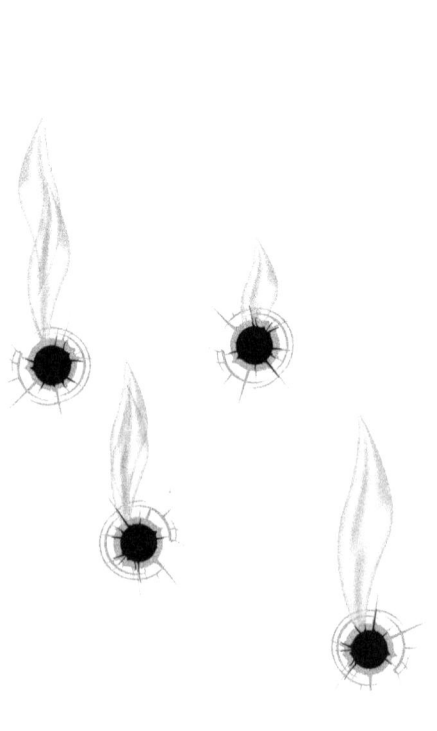

CHAPTER 19

THE NEXT DAY I GOT A CALL from Marshal Palmer. He invited me out for a drink. I told him to fuck off, as my ribs were still hurting too much to get out of bed.

He kept calling over the next few days. By the third day I finally took him up on his offer, just to get him to leave me alone. It took me nearly an hour to get across town to meet up again at the Bullpen bar by the stadium. He thought it would be hilarious to rendezvous at the site of our first date. With Ricker dead he seemed to be in a more cheerful mood.

This time when I walked into the bar, the place was nearly deserted—there was no game taking place at the stadium across the street. The only dregs there were Palmer—at a table by himself with a newly poured beer—and a college girl behind the bar, who was spending more time studying for an exam than paying attention to any customers.

I grimaced when I sat down—my ribs and back still hurt. Palmer chuckled and downed some of his beer.

"I was going to order you one, on me. But I'm guessing you're loaded up on painkillers, so maybe alcohol isn't the best thing at the moment."

"Yeah, yeah—laugh it up. Let me give you a couple of whacks to the ribs and see how joyful you are about it."

"That's no way to talk to a friend."

"Who said that I was your friend?"

He kicked a bag that was under the table, and I felt it flop over onto my foot. "A gift from Ms. Burkhart. That's what kind of friend I am."

"Gee, thanks," I spat back. "You must be thrilled at how all of this turned out. Probably saved you a lot of paperwork."

"How all of what turned out?" He was trying to play dumb. It didn't suit him.

"You know what I mean."

"No, I don't. If you're asking about my investigation into the white supremacist leader known as Ricker—it appears he has disappeared from the radar. Really, we had no hard evidence against him, just on the Nordic Hammer crew. With his disappearance, and me without enough evidence to bring up a case, it's most likely I'll have to shelve my investigation and move on to the next case on the list."

"And how does Ms. Burkhart feel about that?"

"Oh, she is much too busy with her outstanding work at the Portland Unity Coalition to get involved in the affairs of a US marshal."

"And the gift in the bag?"

"Just a thank-you between friends."

"But why? She paid me to get rid of him, yet she's the one who pulled the trigger."

"And she couldn't have done it without you. You got the man she was after out into the open. I've been trying for weeks to get any kind of a thread on Ricker, and then you rolled in and got a face-to-face meeting with him, just like that. The man was able to sneak up on a gun-running heroin dealer and kill him in his own house without a fuss. Ms. Burkhart was afraid he could do the same thing to her at any time—especially since the hit on her brother went so disastrously that she was sure Ricker would never dish out the opportunity to blood in someone from his Hammers gang again."

"Maybe I got him out into the open—but how did she find me? I never told anyone where we were meeting."

"She caught up with him at the police station. I informed her what had happened to her employee— I told her about the car chase and Dixon buying the farm. She swung by to pay a visit when she saw someone staking out the place in a black F-150. He looked like he had a rifle in his hands and was aiming at someone who had just walked out of the station door: you."

"I remember that scene. So he really had a gun on me then? I'll be damned."

"She got close enough to hear his end of the conversation and figured out who he was. Even now we don't have a warrant for his arrest. Hell, he played it so cool we weren't anywhere close to having one—not even for the killing of Pete Finn. If she popped him right there in front of a police station she'd be charged for murder in no time."

I tried to think it all over. My head was still spinning from the last few days. "That doesn't answer how she knew to be at the Sellwood Bridge that night. She didn't follow me and I sure as hell ditched your boys."

"She didn't follow you. She followed him."

"What kind of damn army trooper is she?"

"None. She hid her iPhone in the bed of the F-150 when he was staring you down in his scope. Like I said, she was worried about Ricker sneaking up on her, so she had her phone and mine link up just in case. Once connected like that, phones can keep track of each other, as long as their batteries last. She asked to borrow my phone and tracked the truck wherever it went. When it started moving around midnight the other night, she thought it might be the right time to sneak up on Ricker. When she got to the scene at the Sellwood Bridge, she let it play out a little. You got Ricker to show himself, and while he was focused on you, she was able to sneak up on him. So in the end, it was mostly your work that got the job done. Payday earned."

"Well, mine and my partner's."

"What is the plan for him?"

"Don't know. He can't go back east, at least not in that shape. Plus, I don't know what's waiting for him there."

Palmer leaned over to grab a smaller bag, and

pulled out a couple of sheets of paper with fresh ink on them. "Take a look."

"What is this?" I asked, scanning through the paper.

"Applications for a private investigator's license in the state of Oregon."

"What the hell am I going to do with this?"

"I talked to your partner the other day in the hospital. Ms. Burkhart was scared enough to have no problem offering up the hundred grand that was really Finn's blood money, but it seemed a strangely specific and high number to demand from her right off the bat. So I did some research on you two. I let your partner know we knew about his prison record in Worcester, Massachusetts, and a few run-ins he'd had in Rhode Island that he didn't think we'd gotten on record. I offered to forget about that if he told me why the demand was so high. He said you two were out here on a job to collect from Finn. Don't deny it—I don't give two shits about it. To be honest, the world is probably a better place with Finn underground too."

"What happened to due process?"

"I didn't pull the trigger on anyone. I'm not an executioner, just a noble observer."

"Your mother must be so proud."

"So I figure that the gift at your feet gets you off the hook from what you came out here for. And your partner isn't going anywhere, so why should you?"

"What are you getting at?"

"You want to go back to a boss calling you night and day for his money? Or do you want to start working for yourself, like in the American dream? To be honest, watching you work has been a treat for me. You know how to hunt down your target, even in a city 3,000 miles away. You're damn good, despite that line about being a bounty hunter from Texas. Hell, I bet you would be really good at it."

"I thought bounty hunters weren't legal in Oregon."

"They aren't, but PI's are. And it's big state. And Portland is a growing city, with people who are all about cultural inclusiveness, pride, love, and a yearning for Bernie Sanders. That likely includes a number of newbies who think Portland is a great place to jump warrants from other states—making it a US Marshals Service territory. But with Portland police struggling to keep up, and me using all my favors to take down the Hammers, I'm out of friends when I need some dirty work done."

"You're a terrible Raylan Givens."

"And you're a shitty Chili Palmer, but you could still use your powers for good. Both you and your partner. I've got plenty of cases on my desk, and I could sure use people like you to help put those files into the closed bin."

I thought it over for a while, looking through the papers. With the money at my feet, Anderson and I were free from our bosses back east. Maybe it was time for a change. "Did you ever get your phone back from Ms. Burkhart?"

The marshal reached into his pocket and waved it around.

"I'll call you with my decision later," I said.

"For now there's some painkillers and a bottle of White Label at my hotel. I'm hoping that's the key to healing bruised ribs."

I hobbled out of the bar slowly and walked to the car, which I had parked in the Goose Hollow neighborhood. I had only been in Portland for a few weeks, but the city was starting to become clearer and clearer to me. I couldn't tell if the death of Ricker and the Nordic Hammers would help stem the tide of racism from outside the city, but inside the bowl of Portland, the sun seemed to shine brighter at that moment than it had a few days ago.

I changed my mind, and instead of heading to the hotel, I went back to the hospital. I had to talk about a business proposal with my partner, Dynamite Anderson.

THE END

CPSIA information can be obtained
at www.ICGtesting.com
Printed in the USA
FSHW020616030919
61662FS